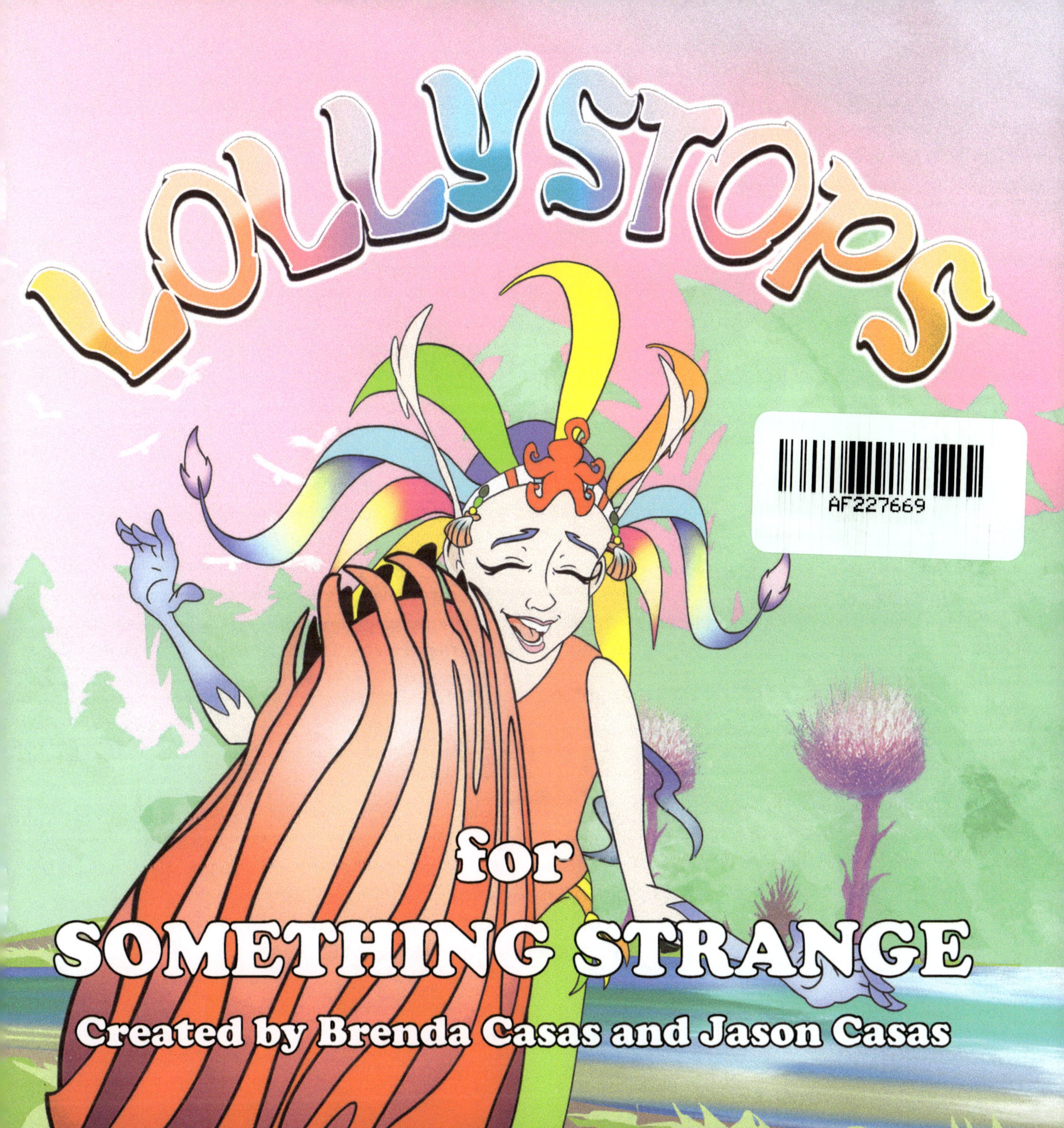

LOLLYSTOPS
for
SOMETHING STRANGE
Created by Brenda Casas and Jason Casas
AF227669

For Abilene & Westyn

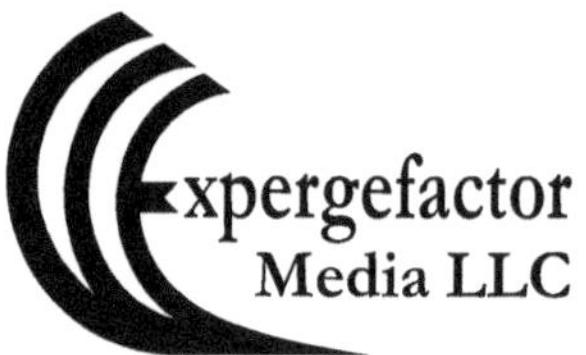

www.lollystops.org

Library of Congress Control Number: 2022900596
ISBN 978-1-7354729-4-2 (Paperback Edition)
ISBN 978-1-7354729-5-9 (Hardback Edition)

Printed and bound in the United States of America
First Edition – February 2022
Published by Expergefactor Media, LLC - Valley Village, CA

Hello, my name is Lolly.
I'm the fairy that cannot fly.

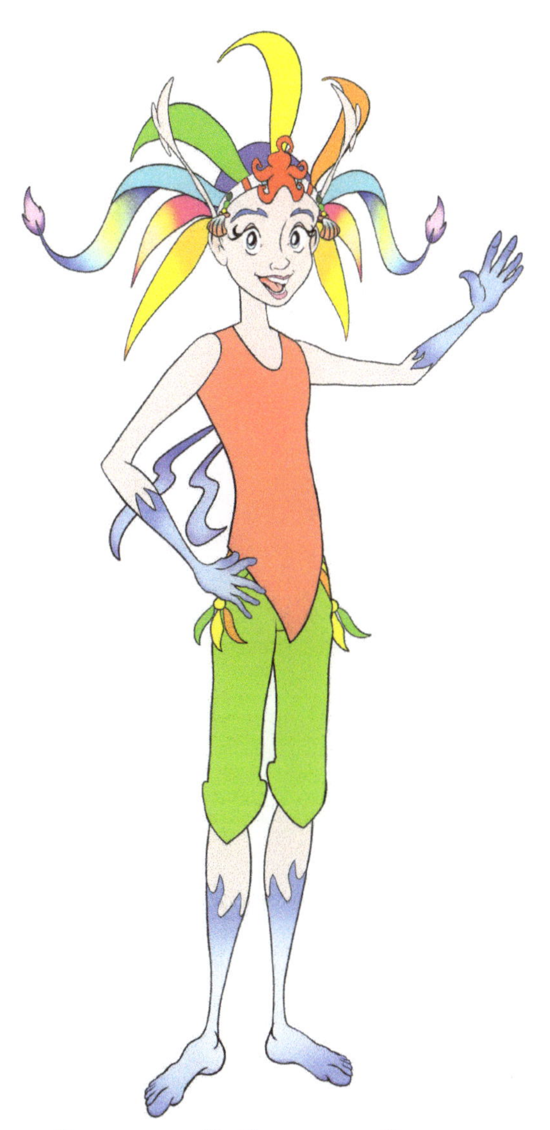

I have lots of fun adventures
when I give new things a try.

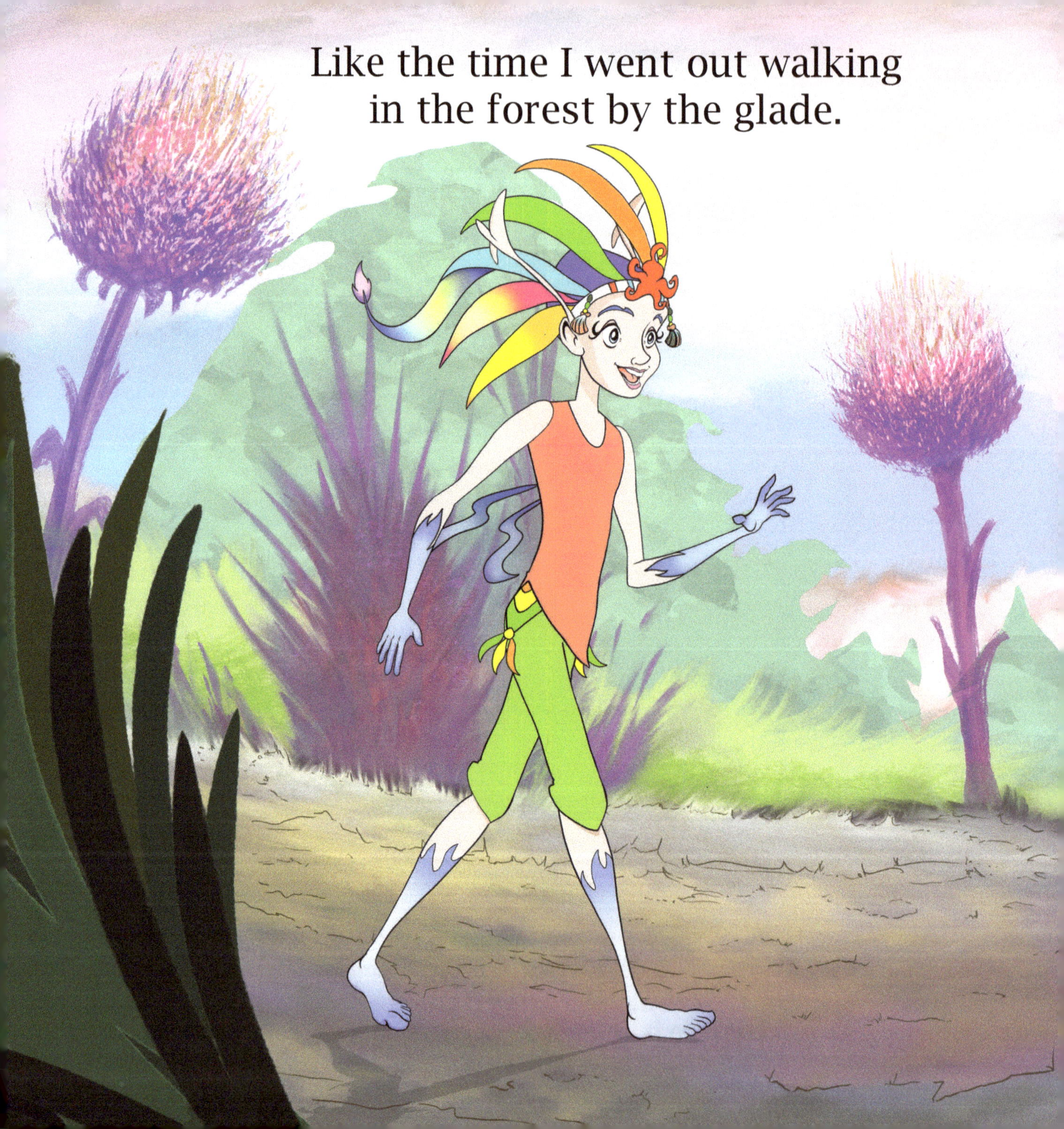
Like the time I went out walking
in the forest by the glade.

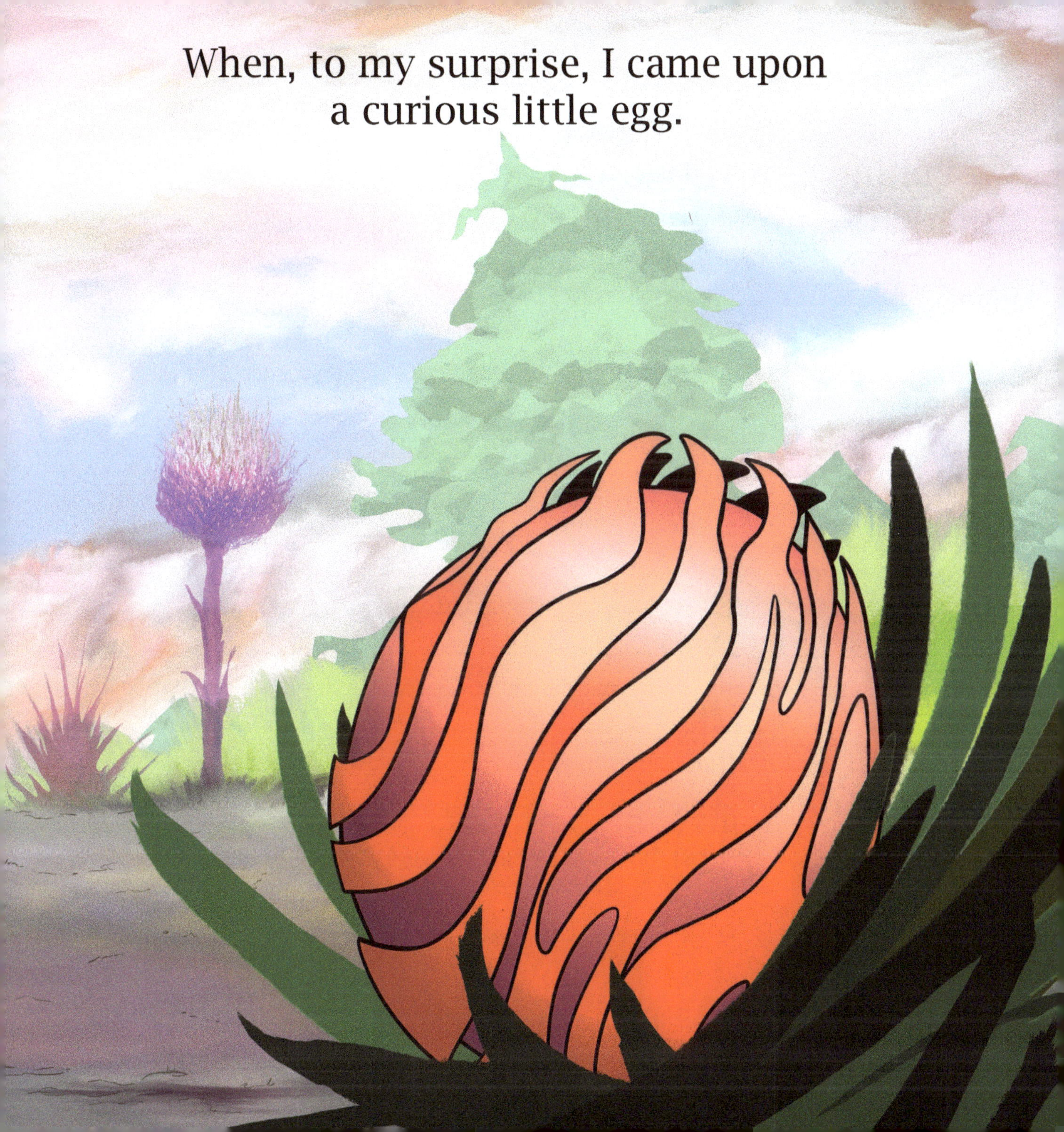
When, to my surprise, I came upon
a curious little egg.

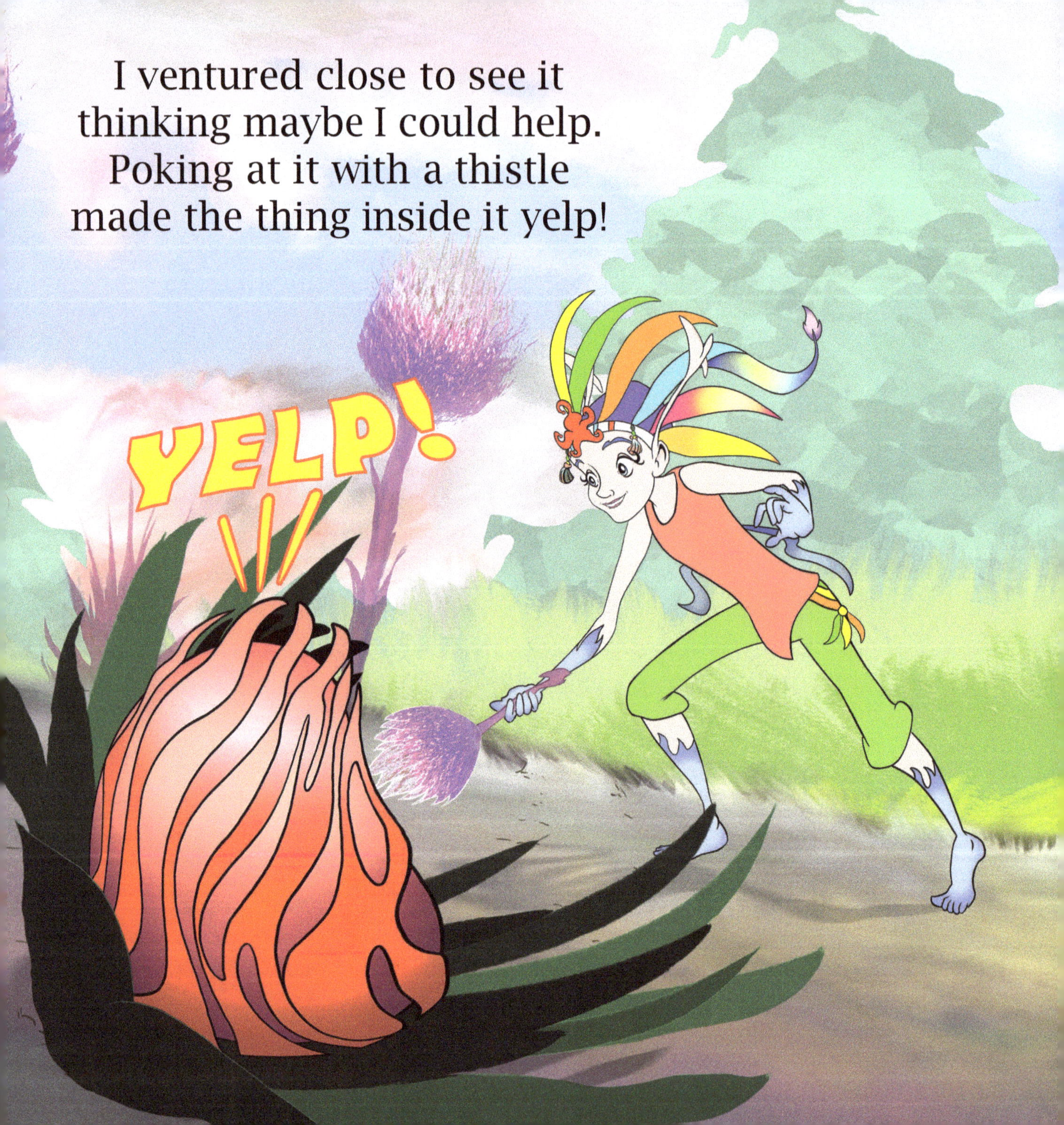

I ventured close to see it
thinking maybe I could help.
Poking at it with a thistle
made the thing inside it yelp!

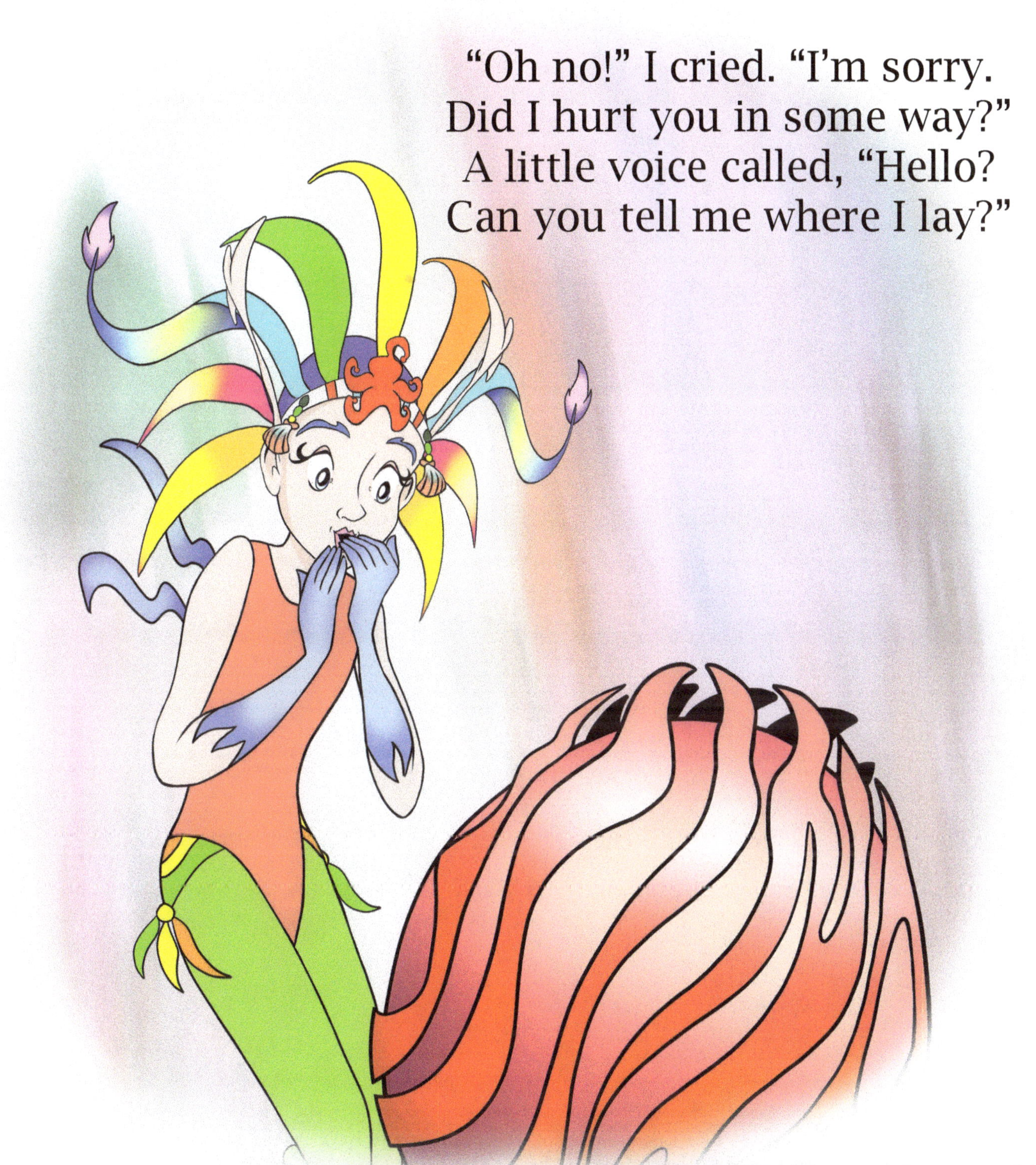

"Oh no!" I cried. "I'm sorry.
Did I hurt you in some way?"
A little voice called, "Hello?
Can you tell me where I lay?"

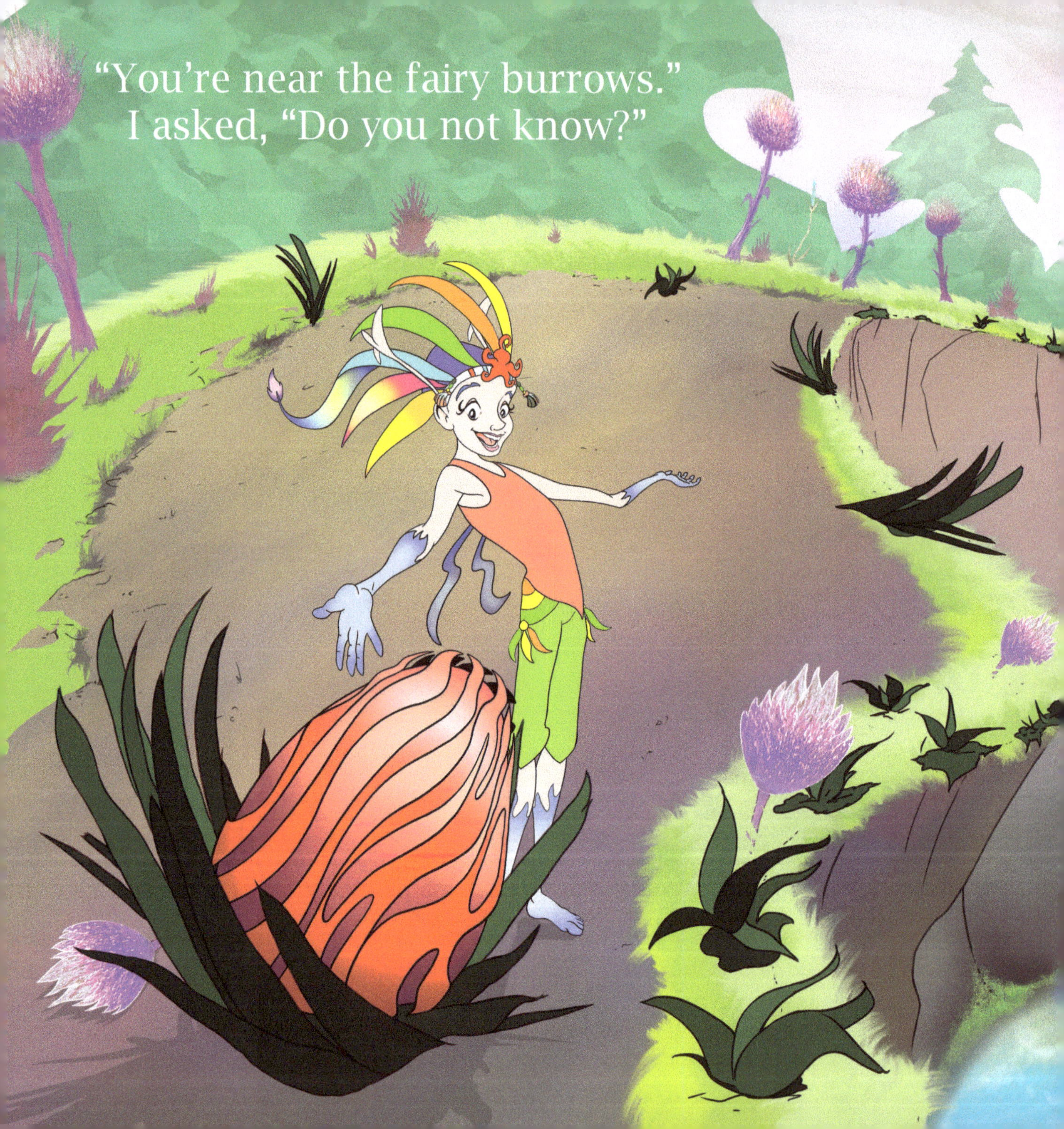
"You're near the fairy burrows."
I asked, "Do you not know?"

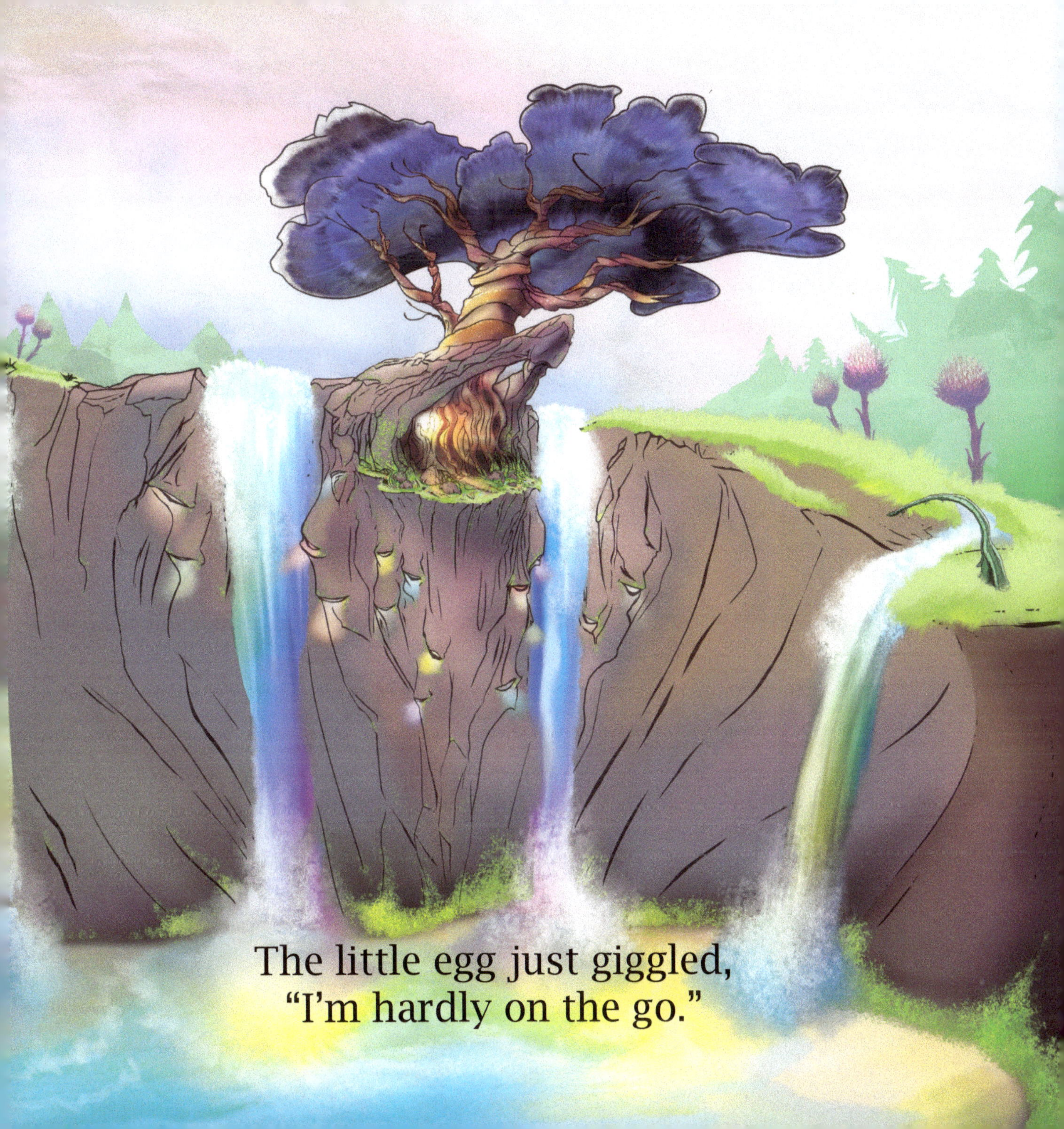

The little egg just giggled,
"I'm hardly on the go."

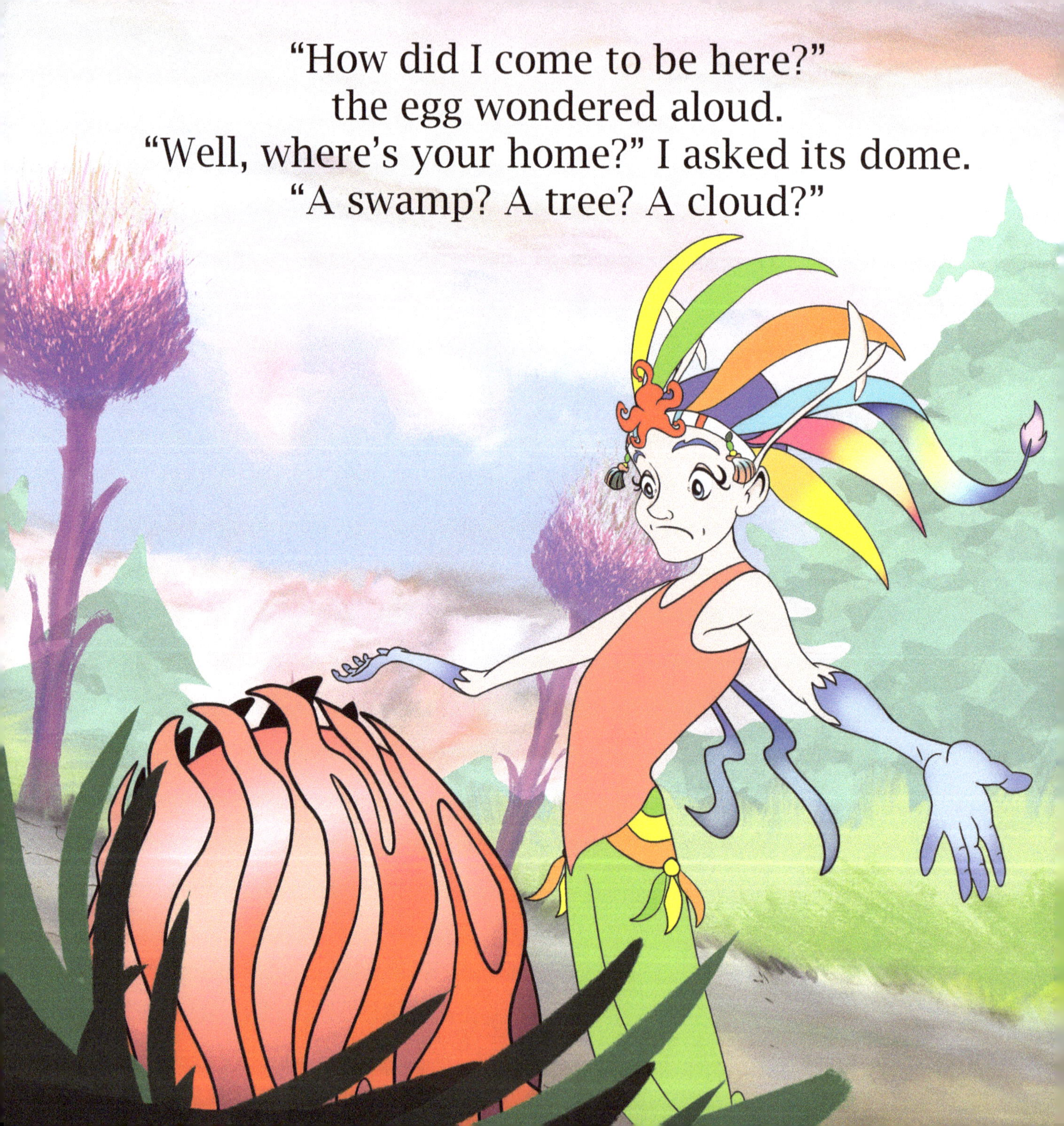
"How did I come to be here?"
the egg wondered aloud.
"Well, where's your home?" I asked its dome.
"A swamp? A tree? A cloud?"

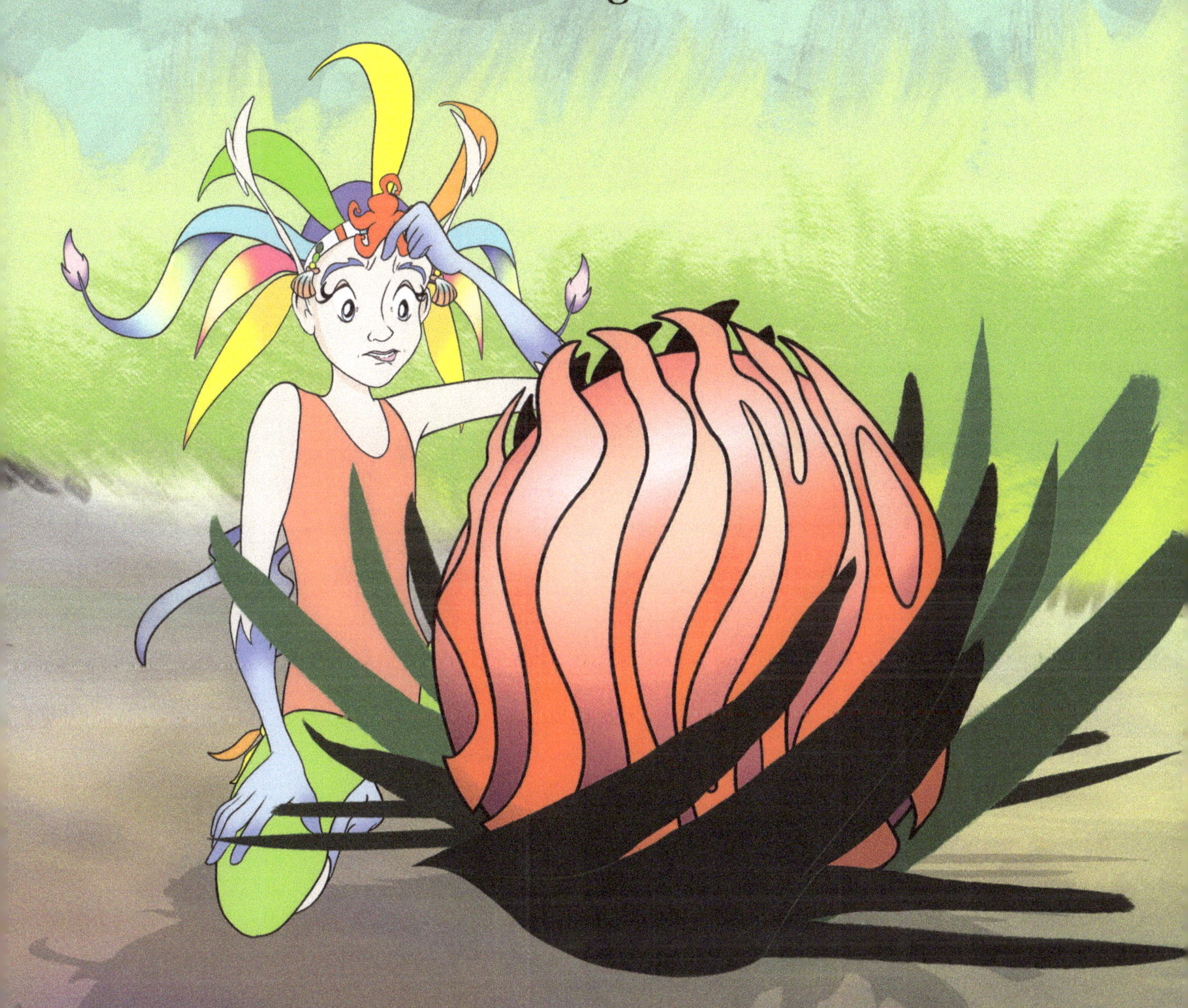

"I just don't know," the egg replied.
"But I'm certain it's not here."
I looked Egg over carefully.
Was this something I should fear?

"Give me a clue?" I tried again.
"Tell me about your mother."
"I couldn't say," Egg sadly said.
"I've never really met her."

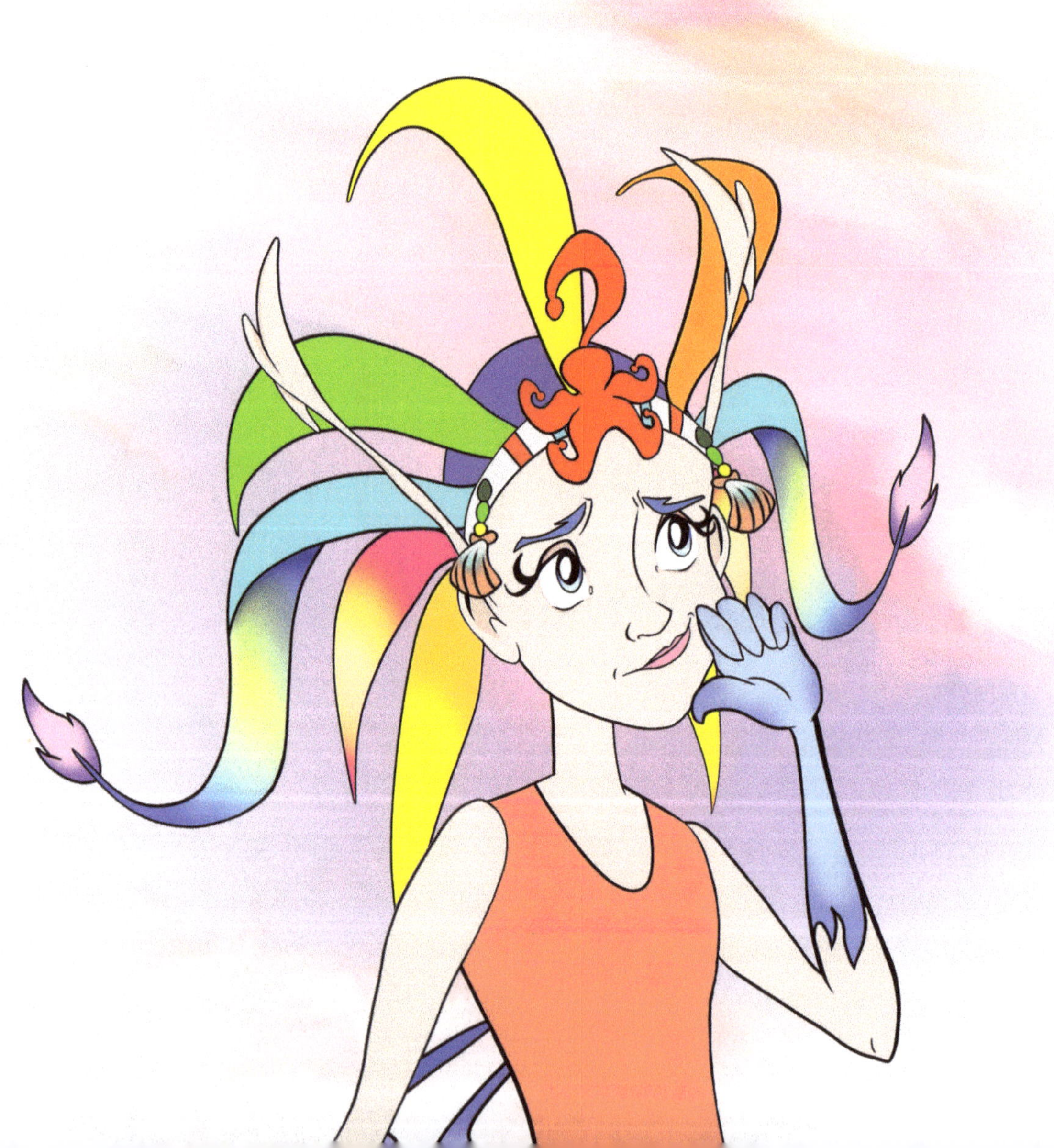

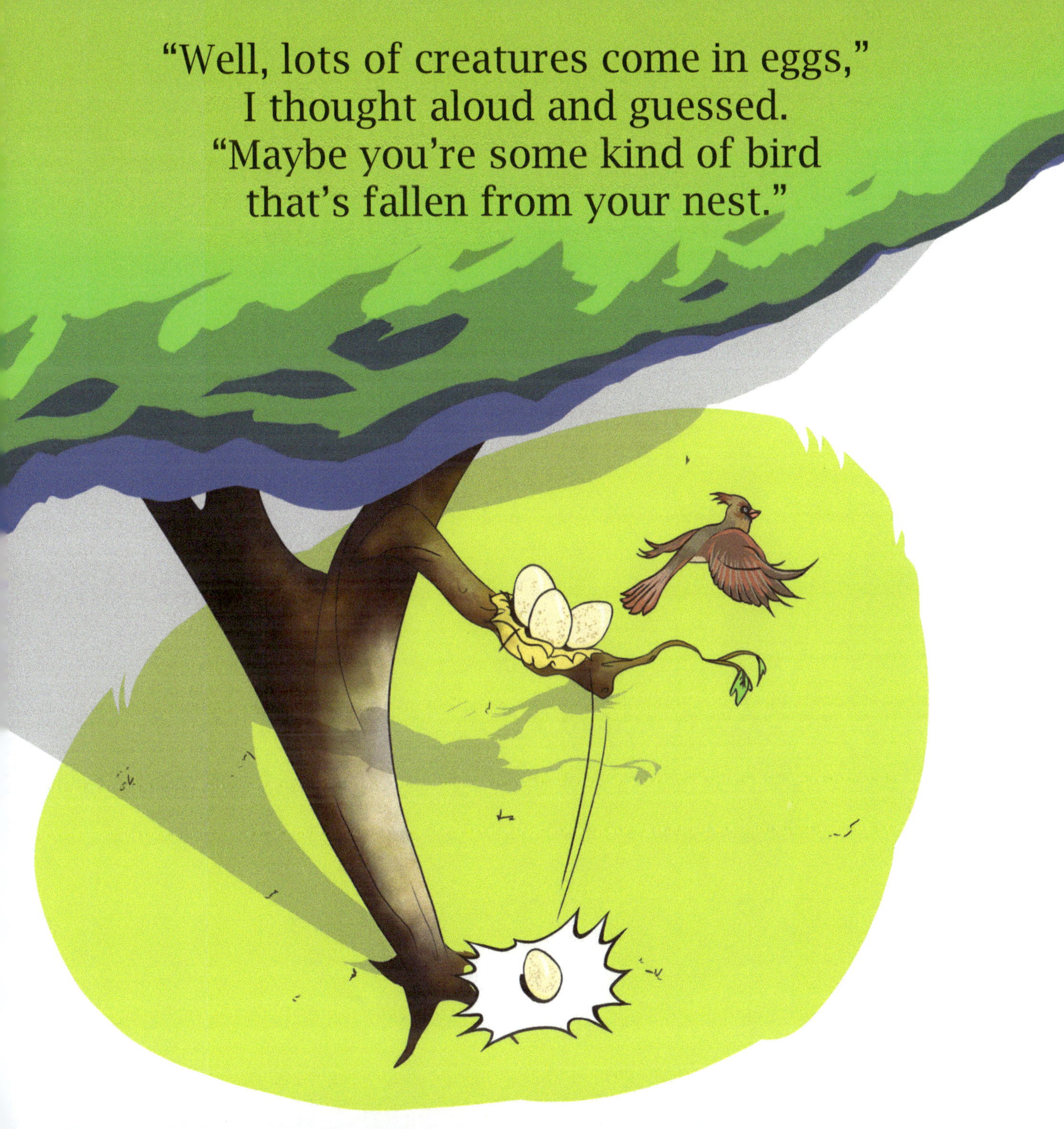

"Well, lots of creatures come in eggs,"
I thought aloud and guessed.
"Maybe you're some kind of bird
that's fallen from your nest."

Egg wobbled in the grass.
It was red, oblong, and round.
"I'm sure I'm not a bird," Egg said.
"A bat? How does that sound?"

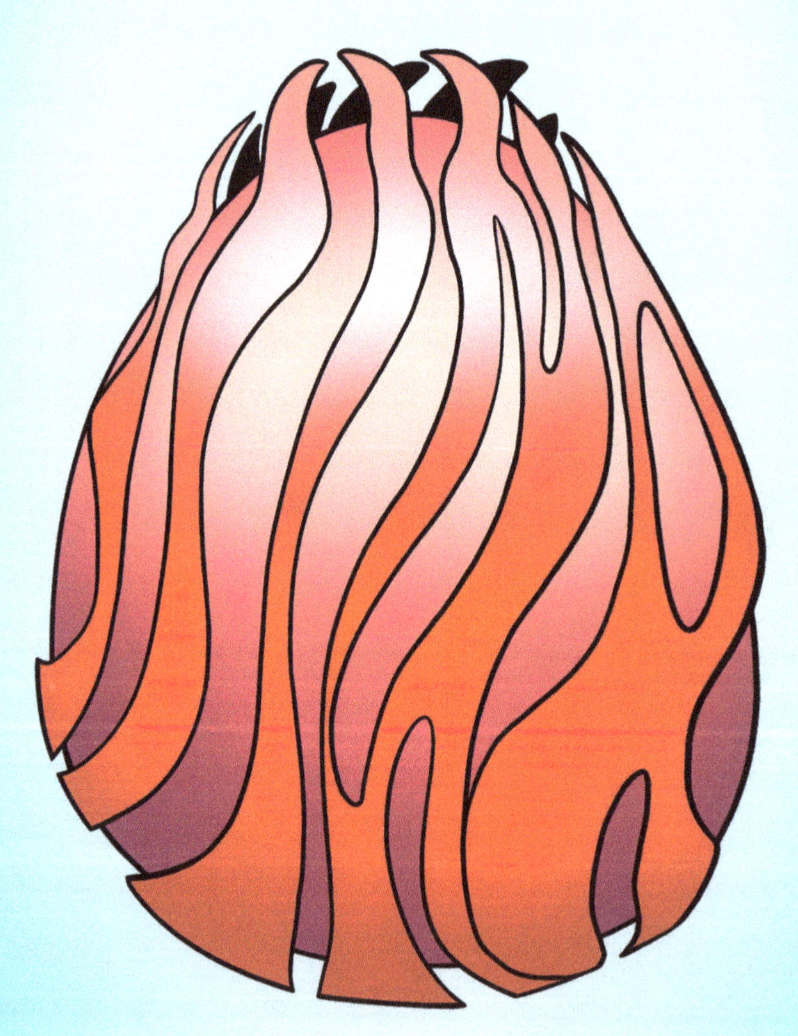

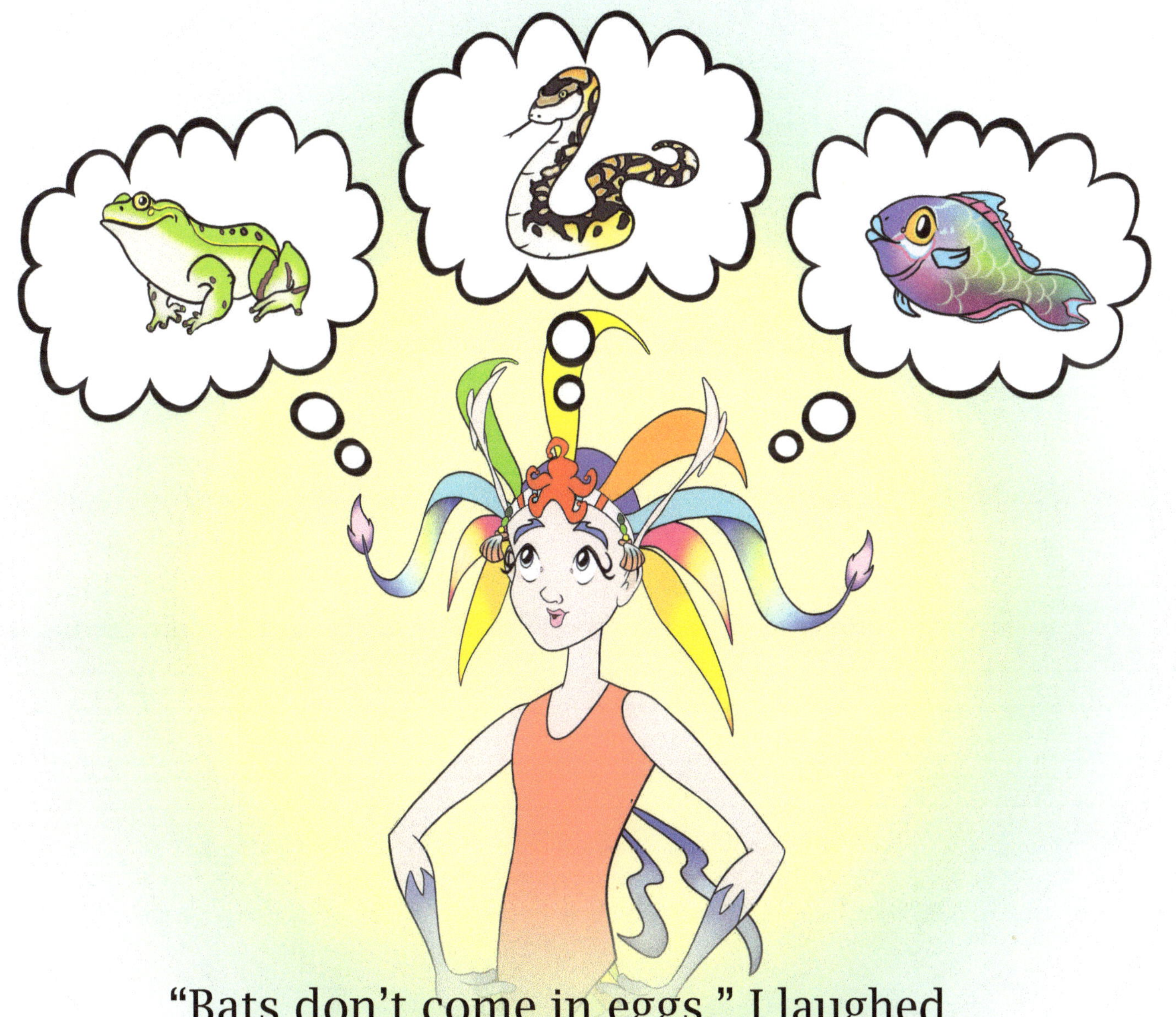

"Bats don't come in eggs," I laughed.
"But frogs, and snakes, and fish do."
Egg sighed, "I don't feel like a frog.
I may be too brand-new."

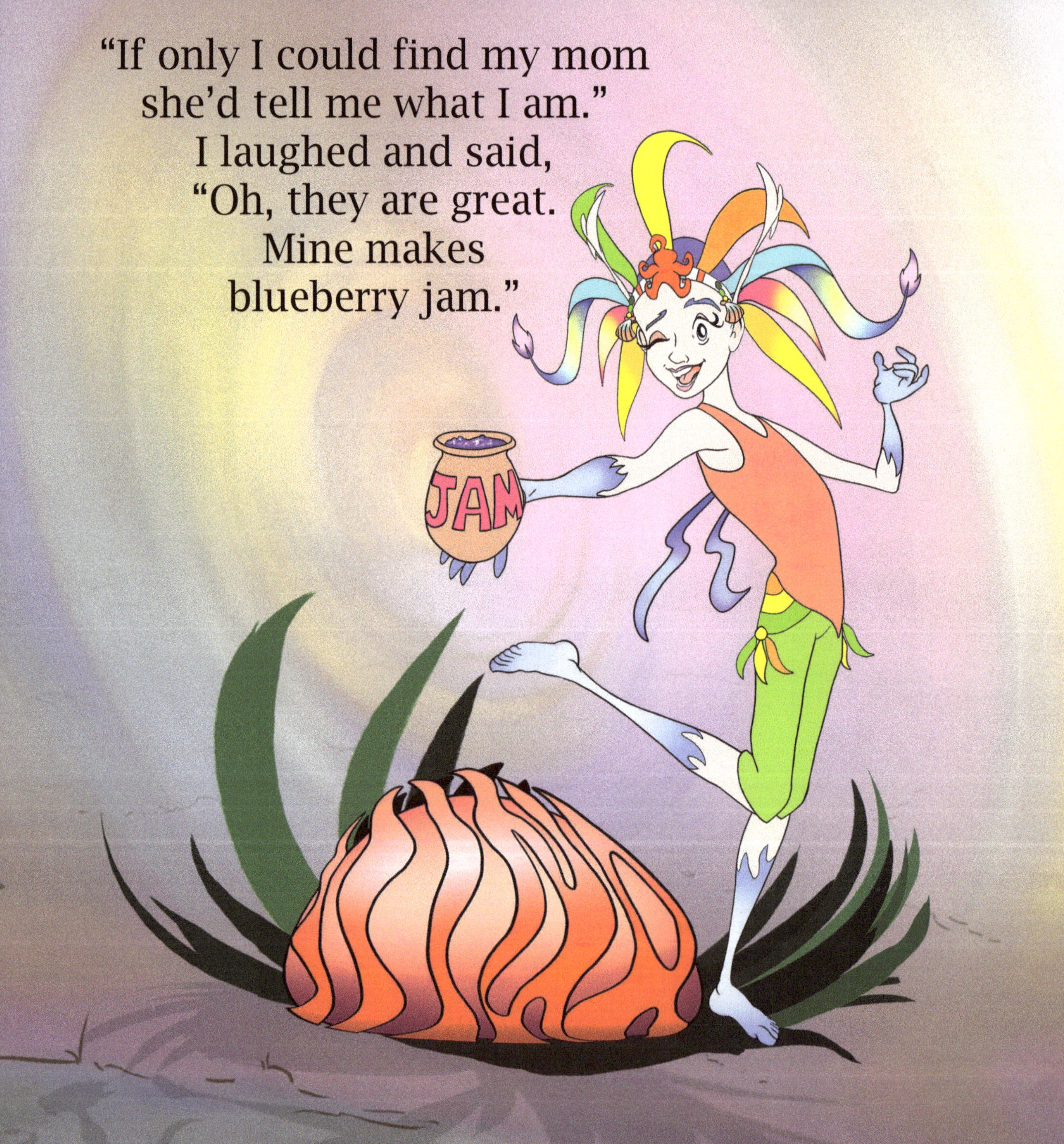

"If only I could find my mom
she'd tell me what I am."
I laughed and said,
"Oh, they are great.
Mine makes
blueberry jam."

"That's it!" I shouted out with glee.
"Our adventure is at hand.
We'll find your mom, no matter what.
We'll search throughout the land."

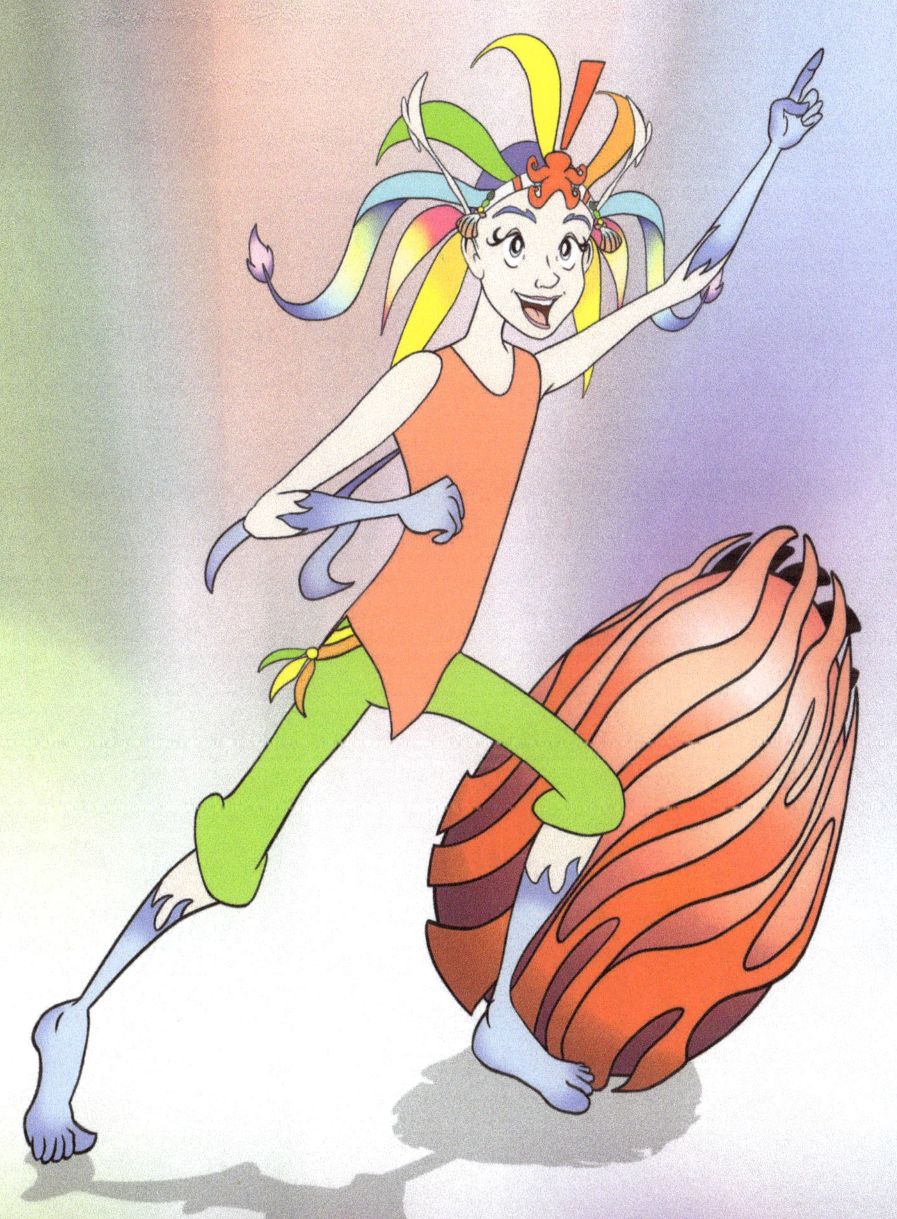

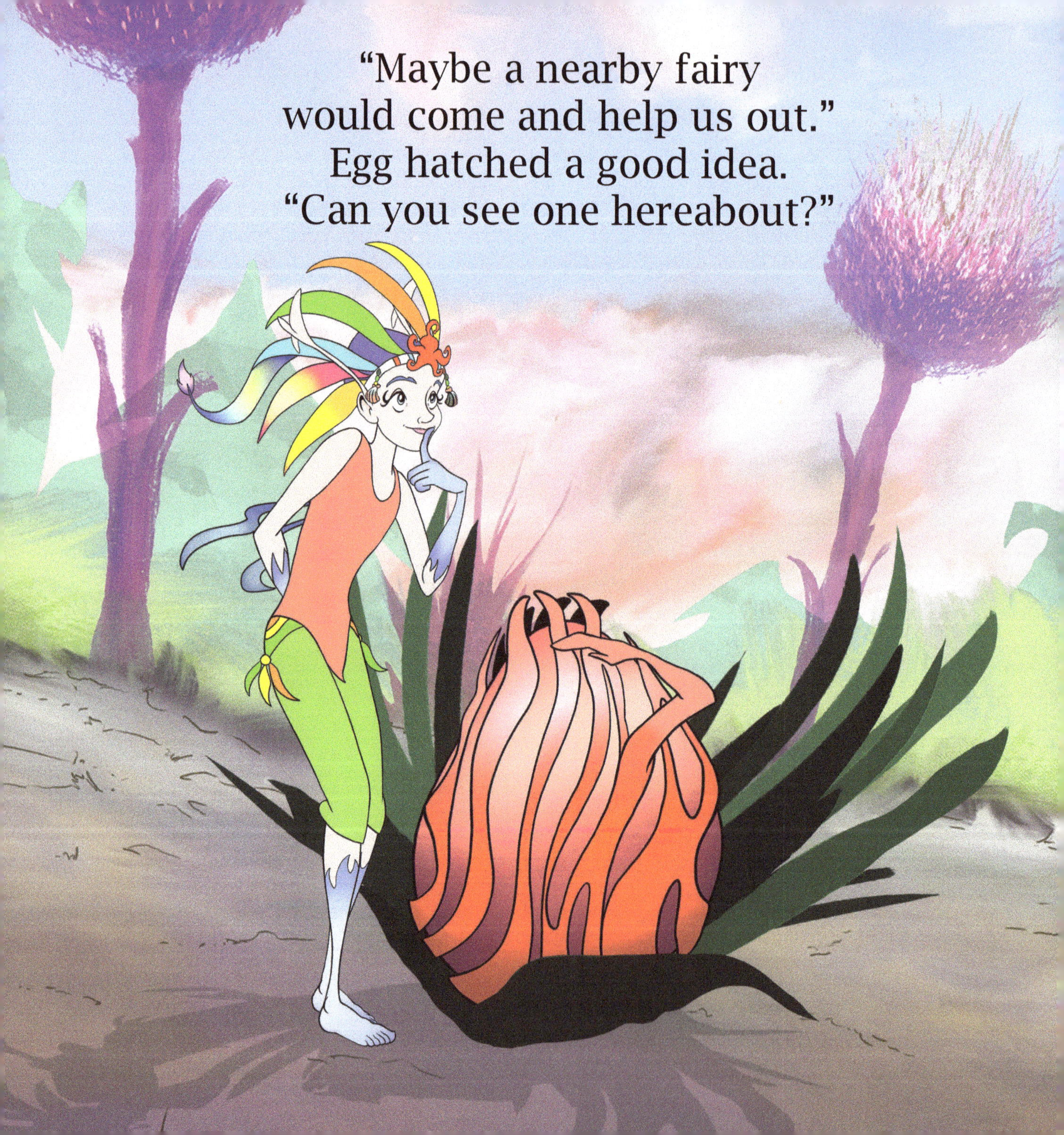

"Maybe a nearby fairy
would come and help us out."
Egg hatched a good idea.
"Can you see one hereabout?"

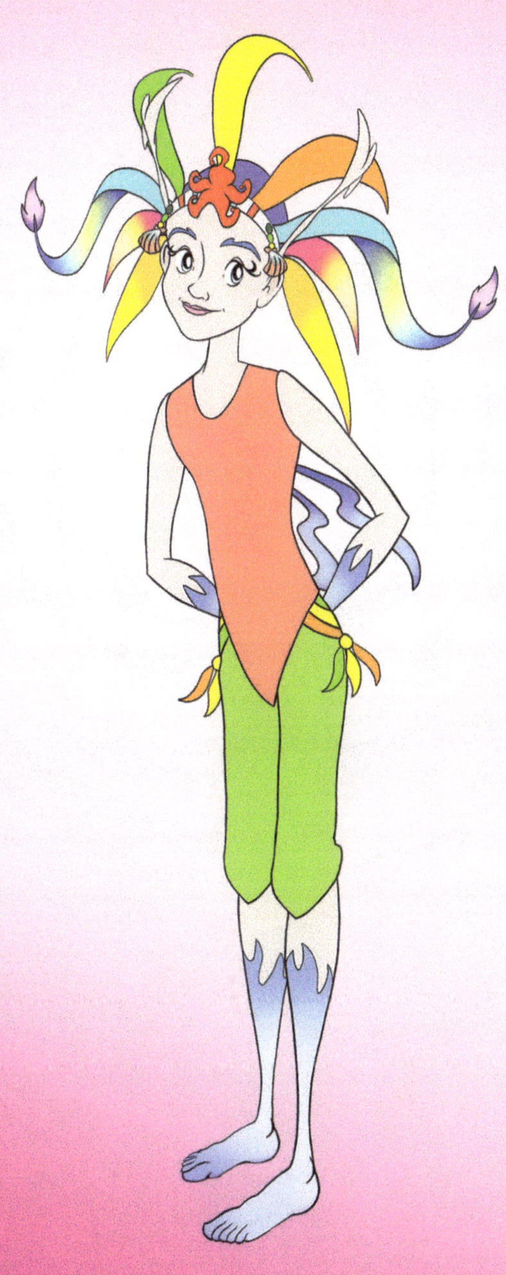

"Why yes, I can,"
I explained to Egg.
"I'm the fairy that
you seek.
I didn't bother
telling you.
See, I'm often
far too meek."

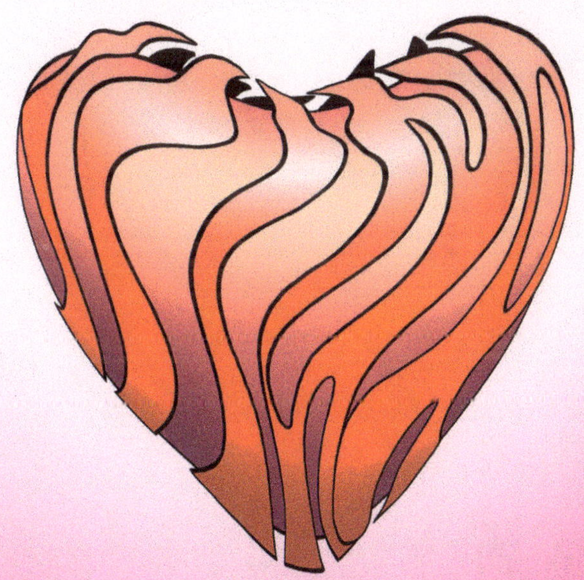

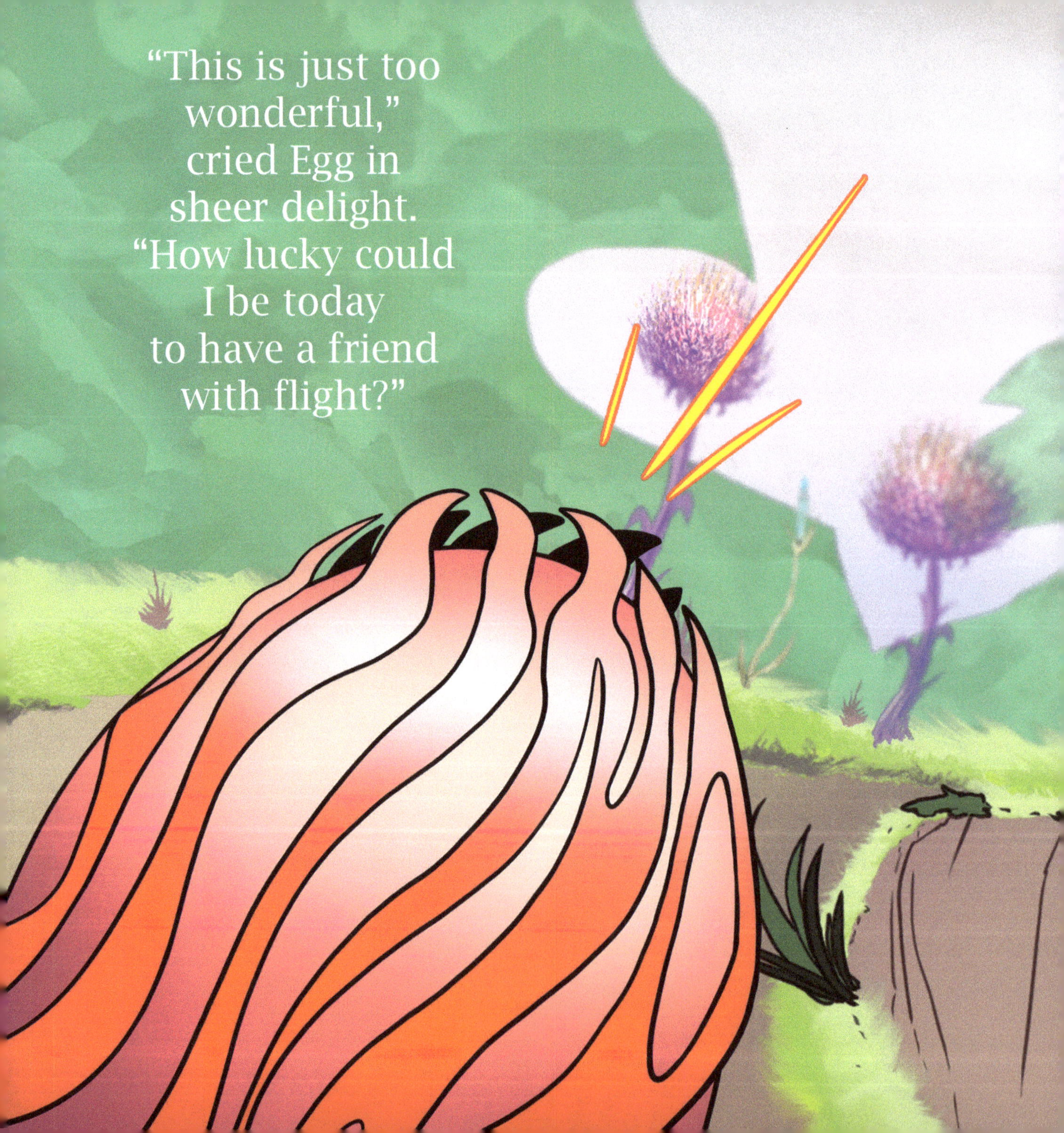

"This is just too wonderful," cried Egg in sheer delight. "How lucky could I be today to have a friend with flight?"

"I don't have flight," I informed my friend.
"My wings, they're not that strong."
"But…" Egg said, then stopped and asked,
"Will you tell me what is wrong?"

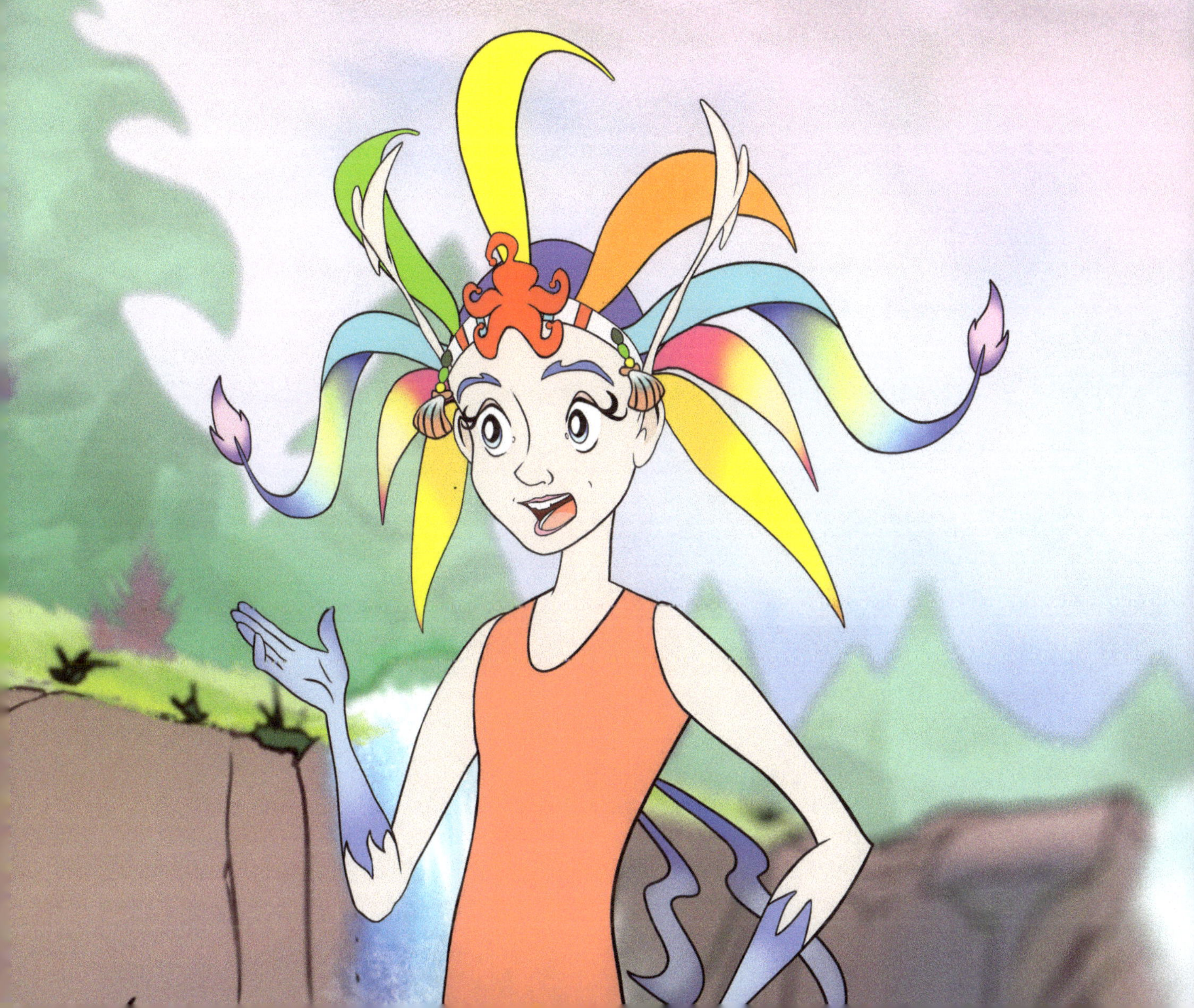

"I try to fly. I really do."
I flexed my wings, though thin.
"I got sick at an early age,
and I haven't flown since then."

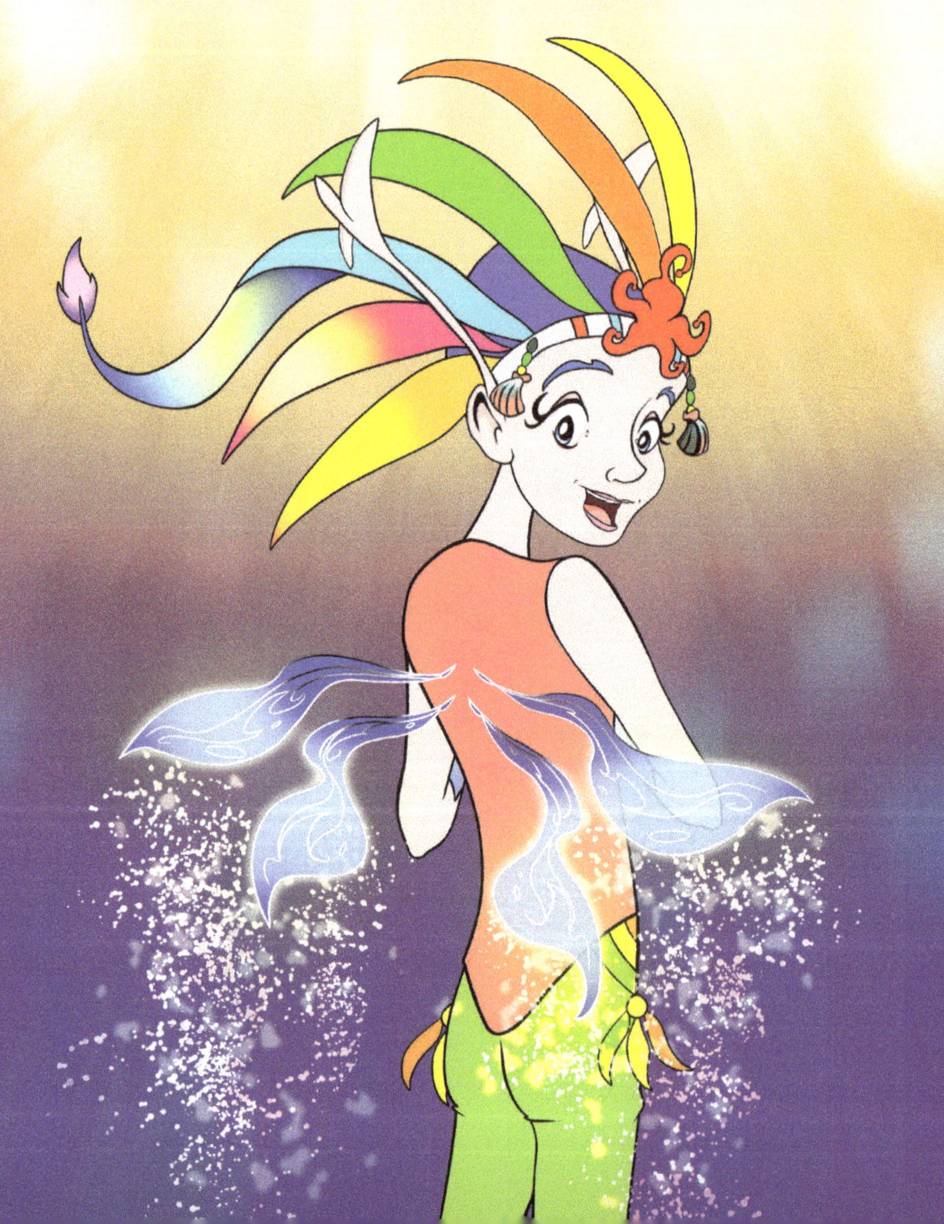

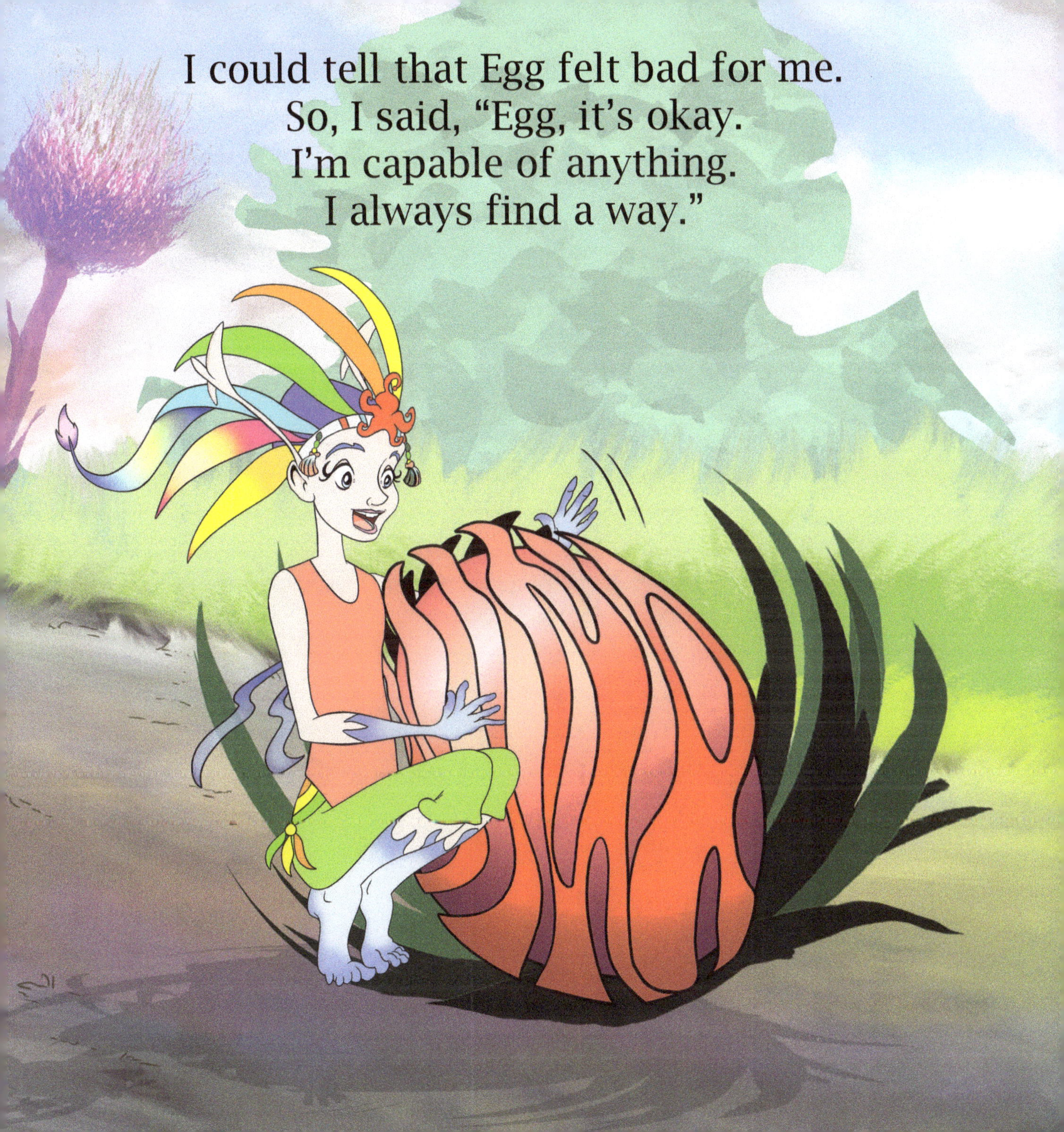

I could tell that Egg felt bad for me.
So, I said, "Egg, it's okay.
I'm capable of anything.
I always find a way."

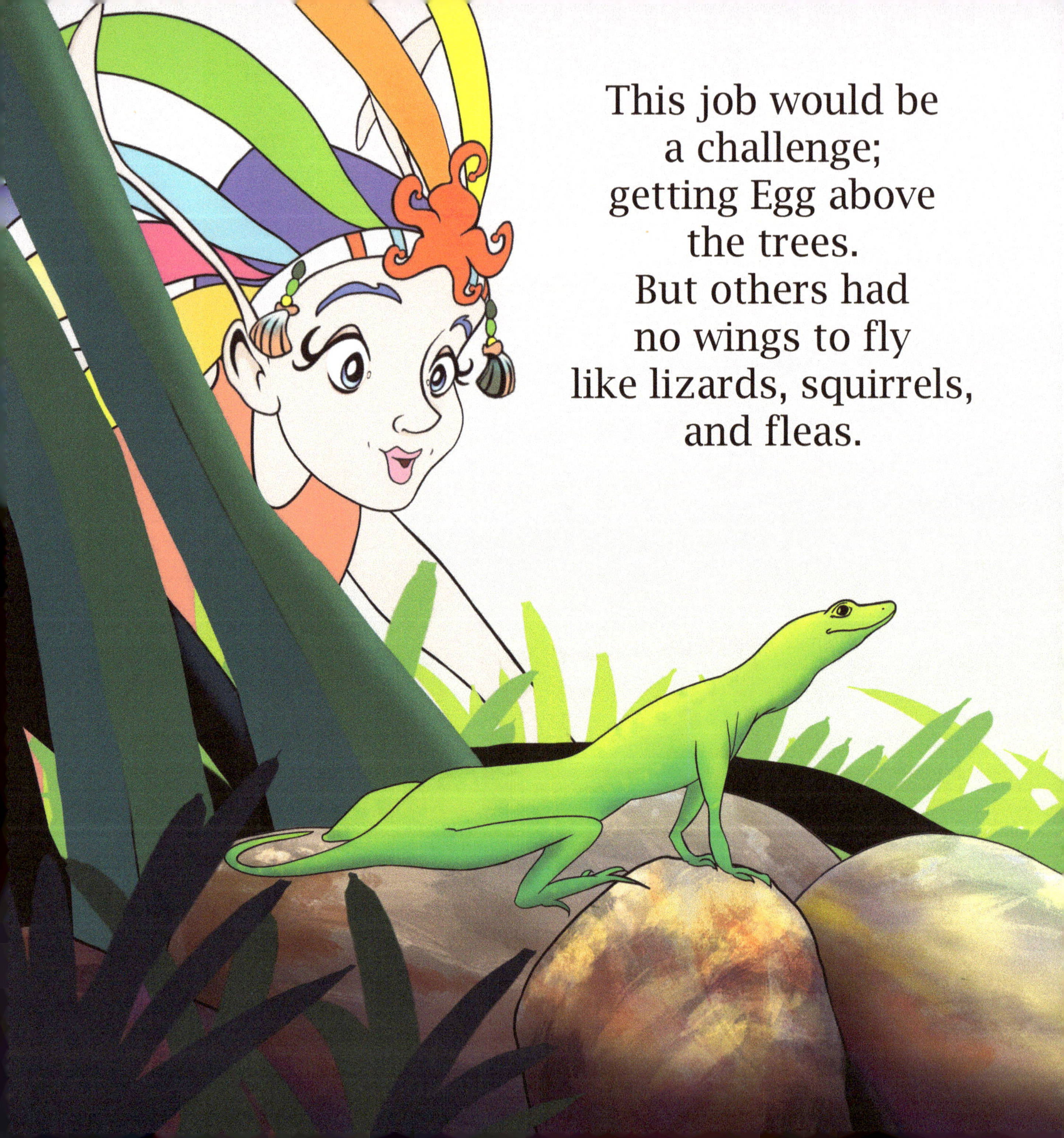
This job would be
a challenge;
getting Egg above
the trees.
But others had
no wings to fly
like lizards, squirrels,
and fleas.

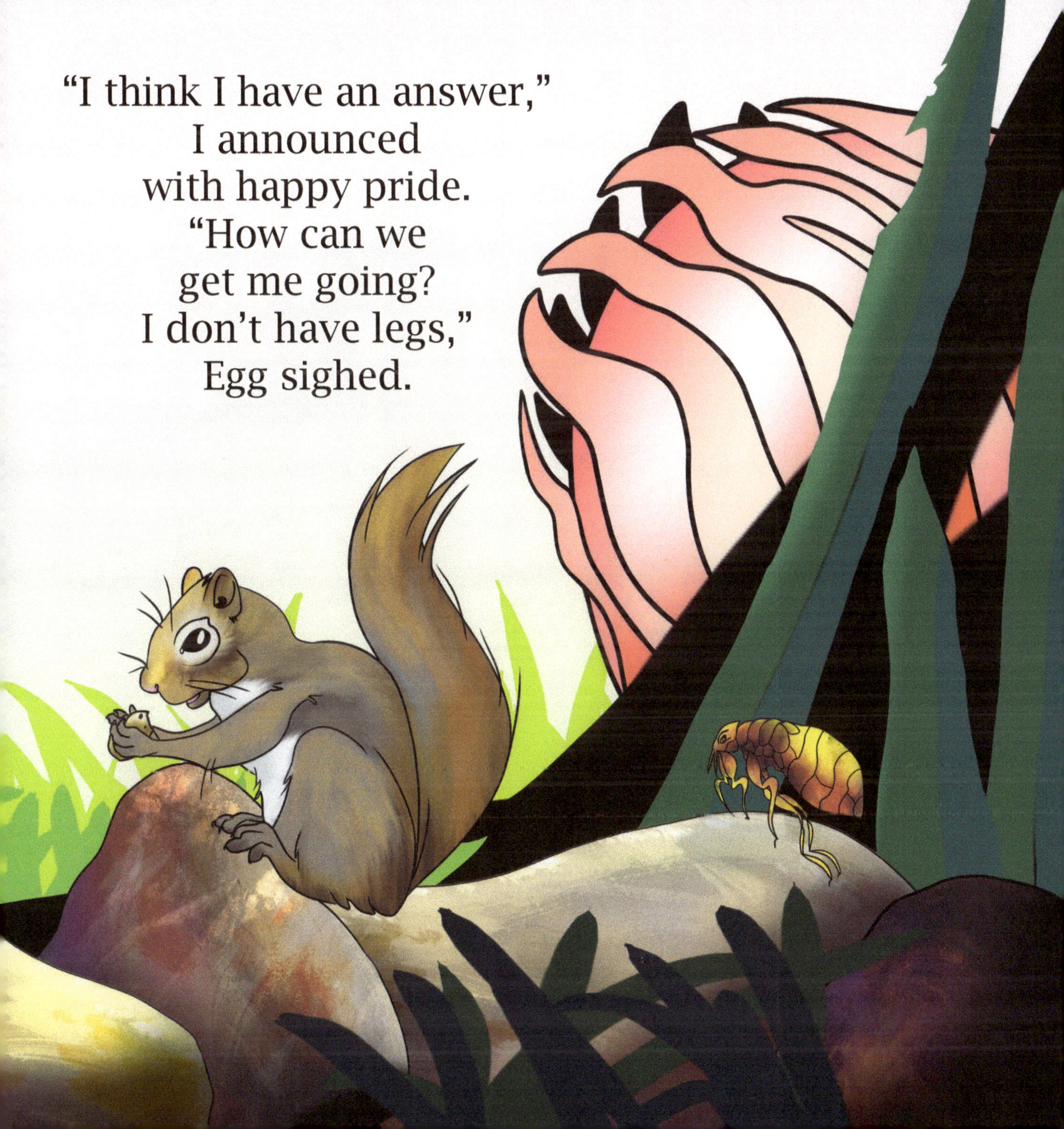

"I think I have an answer,"
I announced
with happy pride.
"How can we
get me going?
I don't have legs,"
Egg sighed.

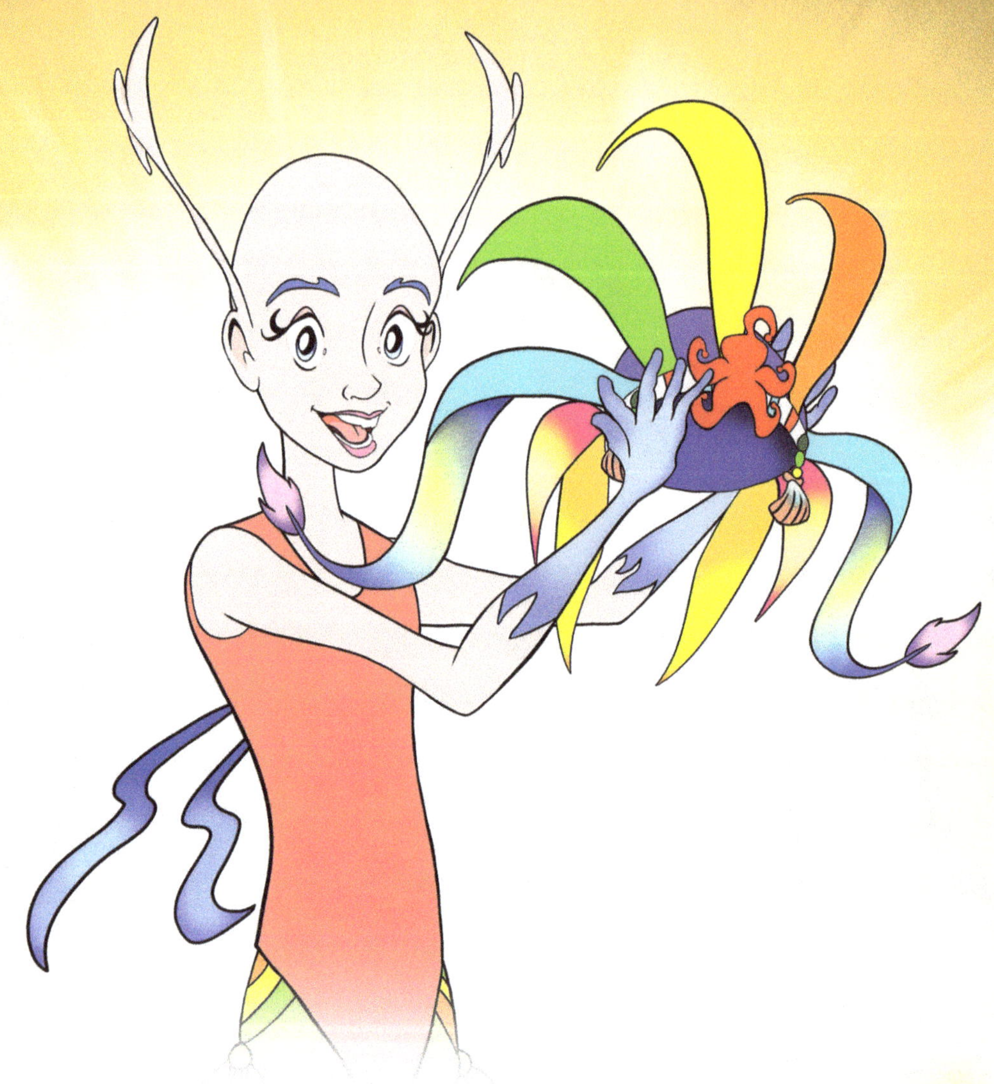

Adjusting my favorite lolly-top,
my headdress—I don't have hair.
That illness that I spoke of;
it even got me there.

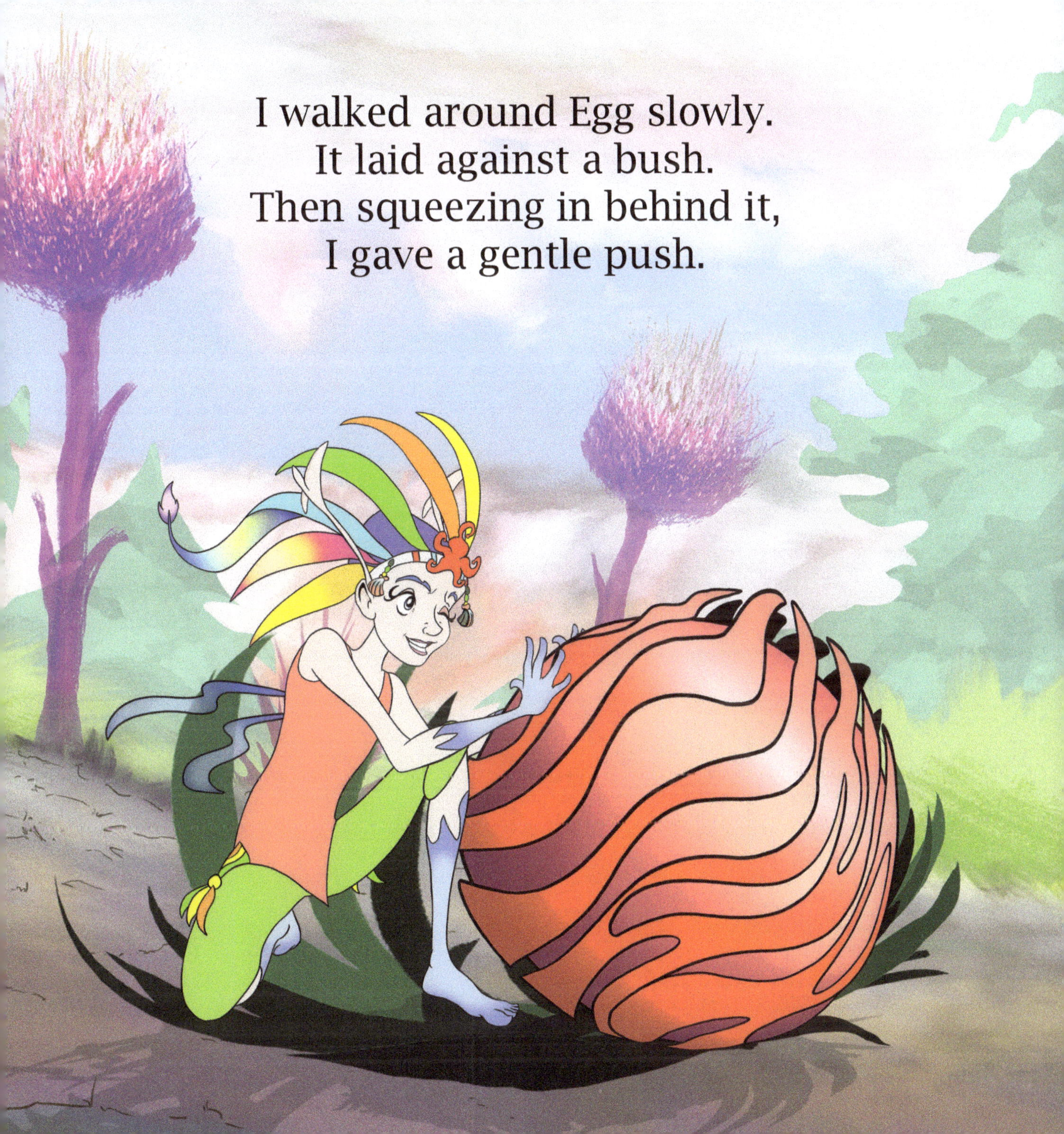

I walked around Egg slowly.
It laid against a bush.
Then squeezing in behind it,
I gave a gentle push.

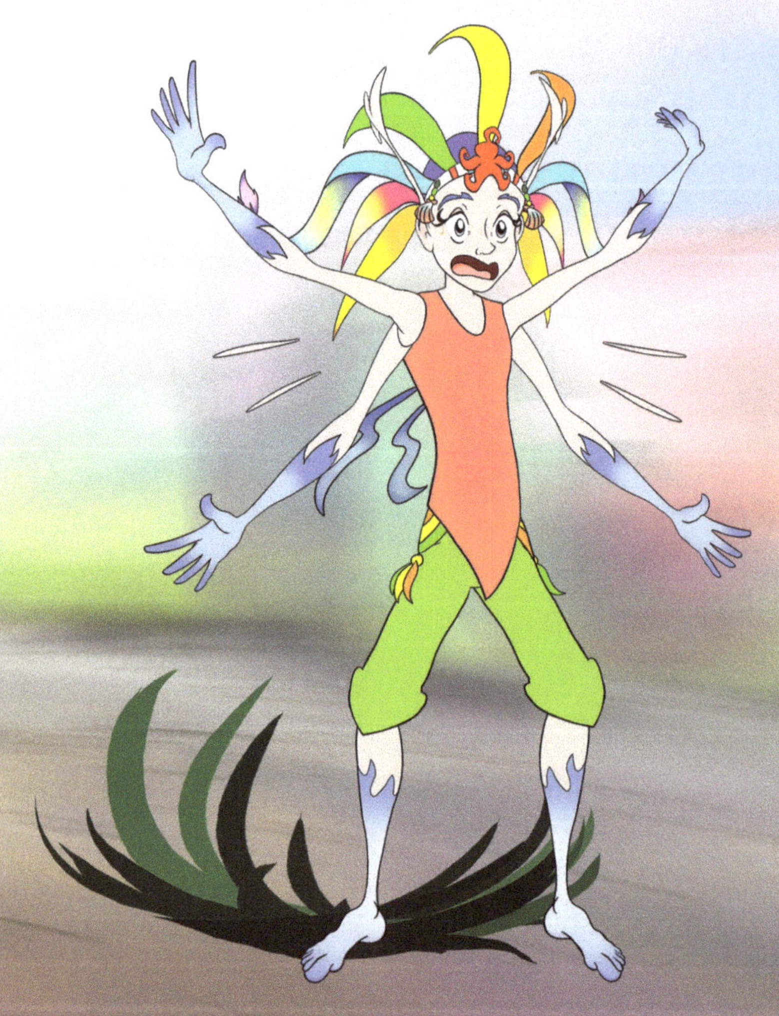

The slope was higher than I thought
and Egg went tumbling down.

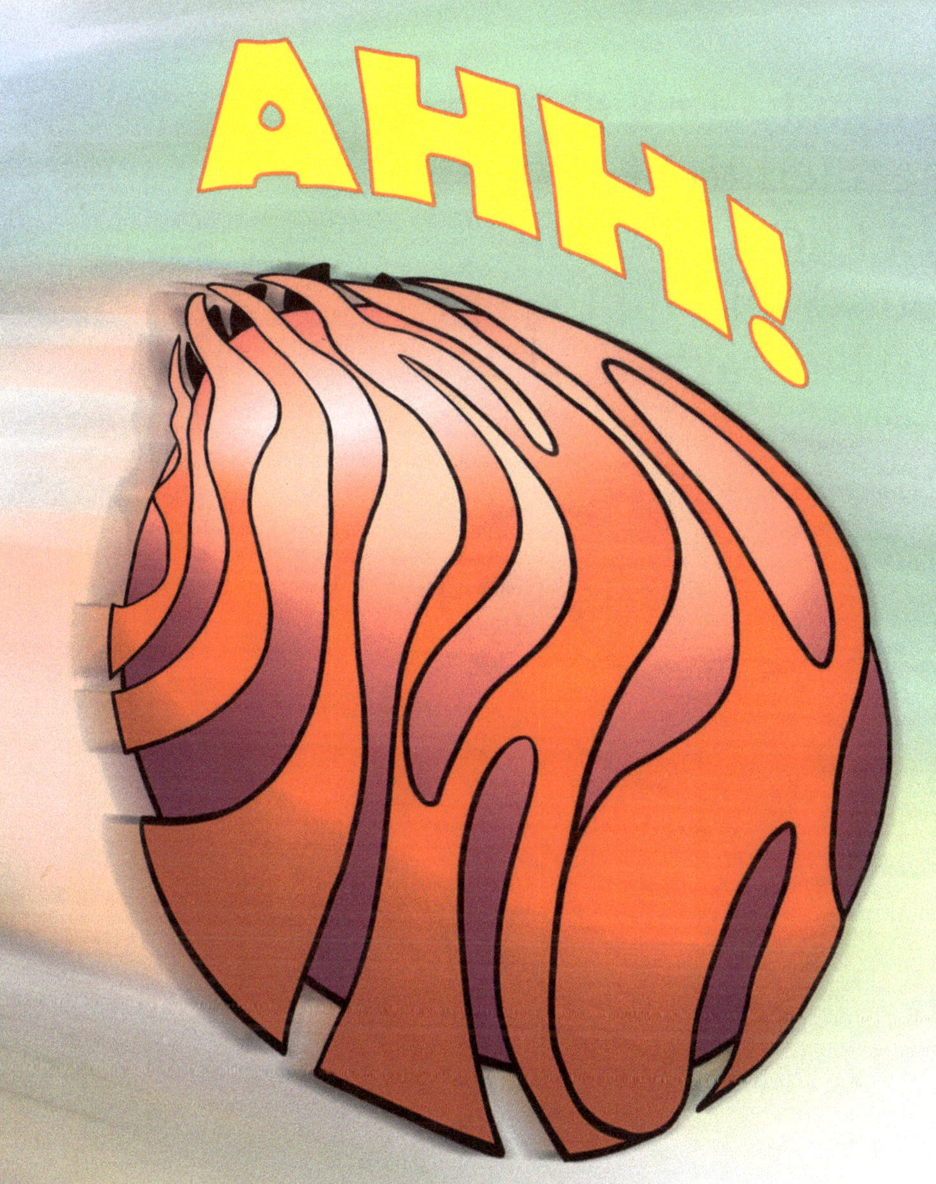

"Ahh!" Egg cried, rolling away
so far across the ground.

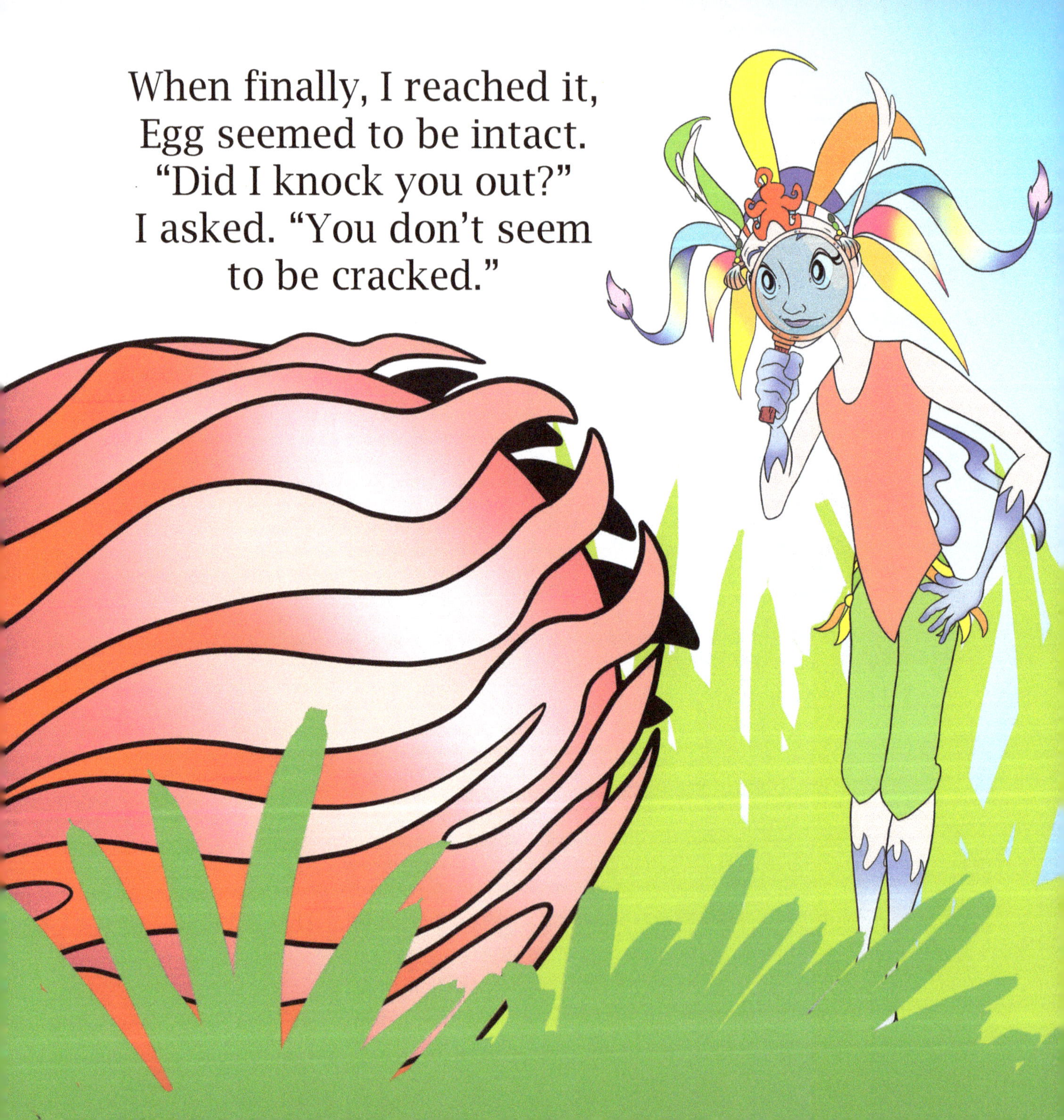

When finally, I reached it,
Egg seemed to be intact.
"Did I knock you out?"
I asked. "You don't seem
to be cracked."

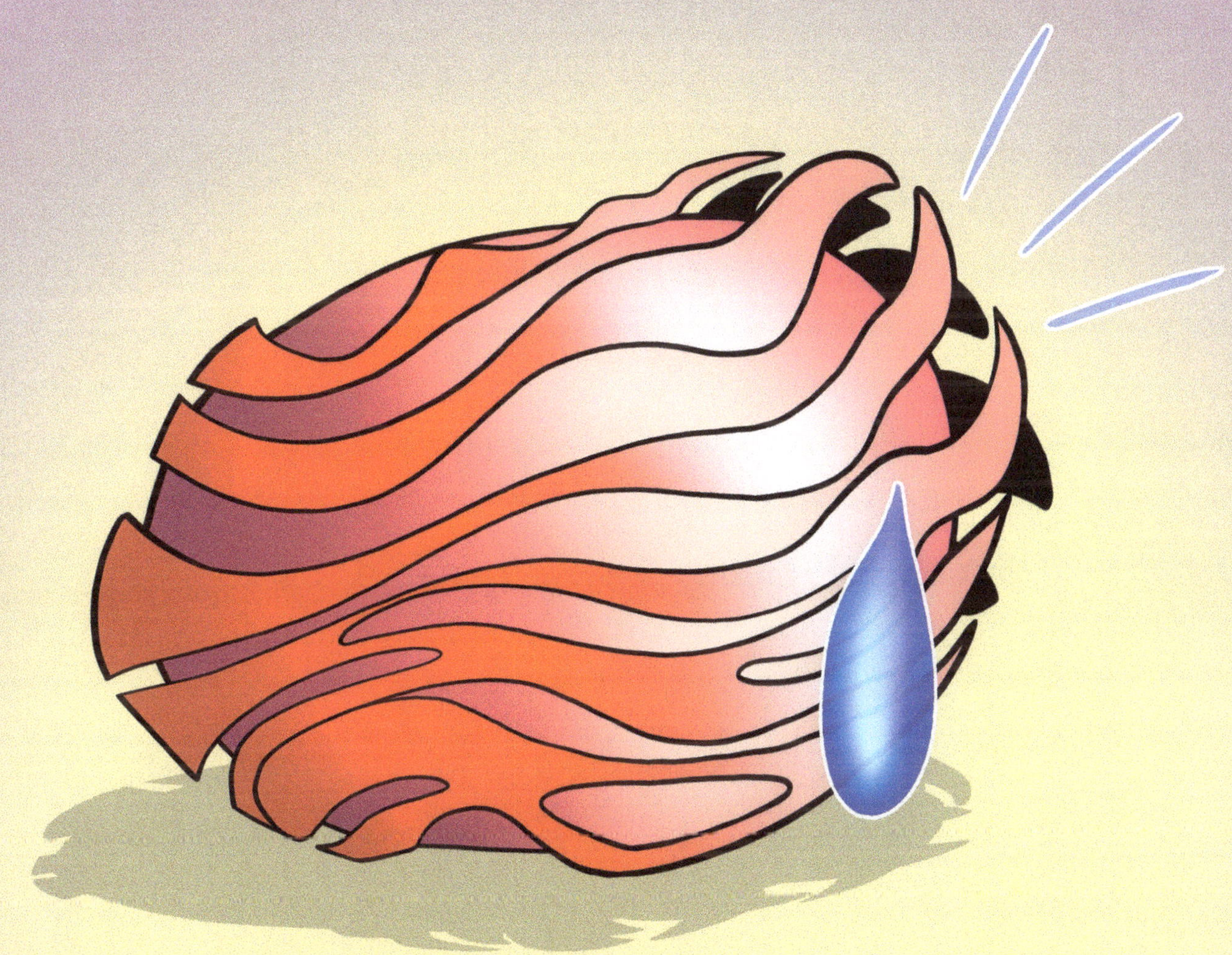

"Um," Egg finally whispered,
"I think I am alright.
But in the future, warn me
so I know to hold on tight."

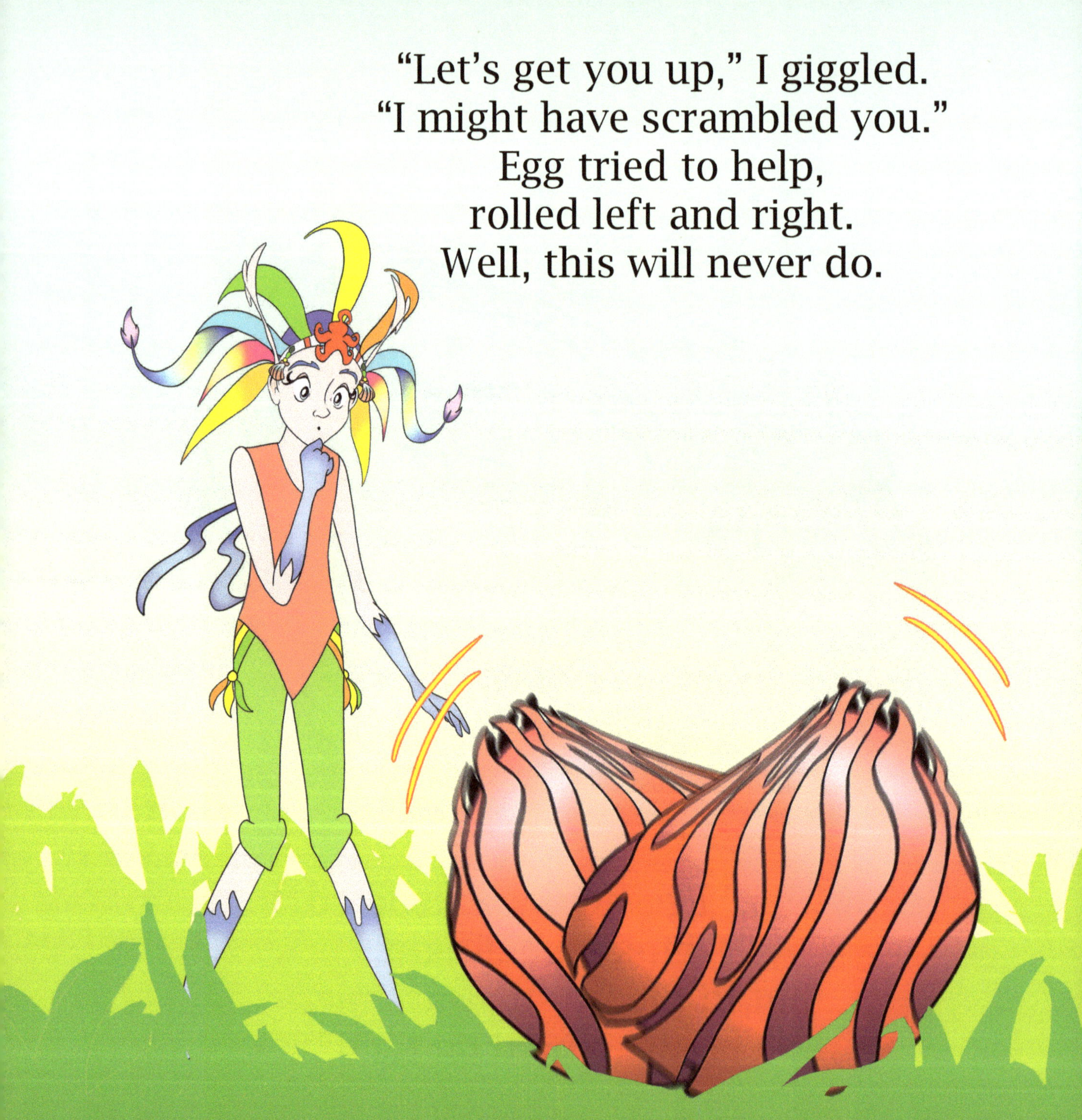

"Let's get you up," I giggled.
"I might have scrambled you."
Egg tried to help,
rolled left and right.
Well, this will never do.

I didn't say that last part.
Egg didn't need to fret.
"We'll get you where you're going.
I'm not done with you yet."

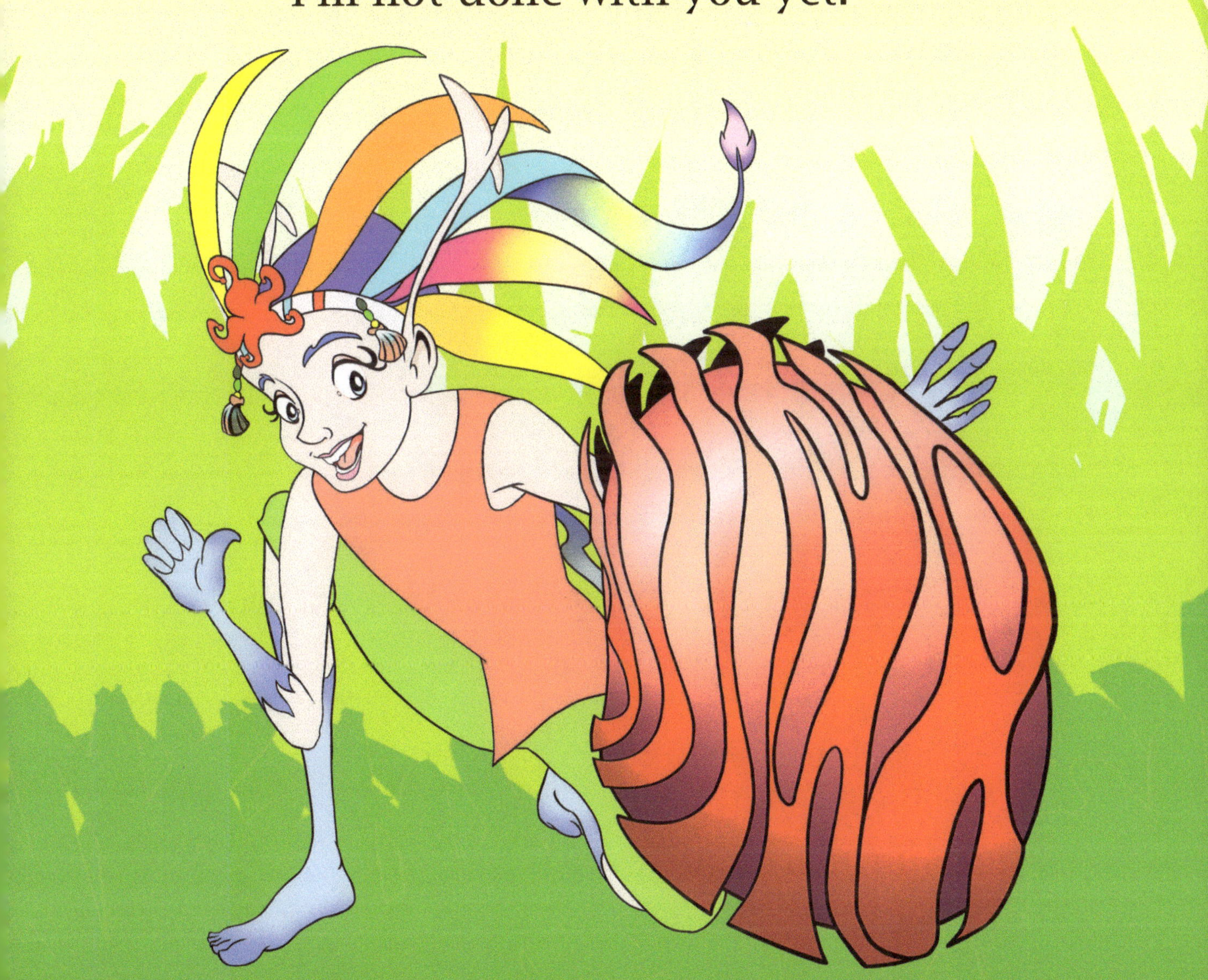

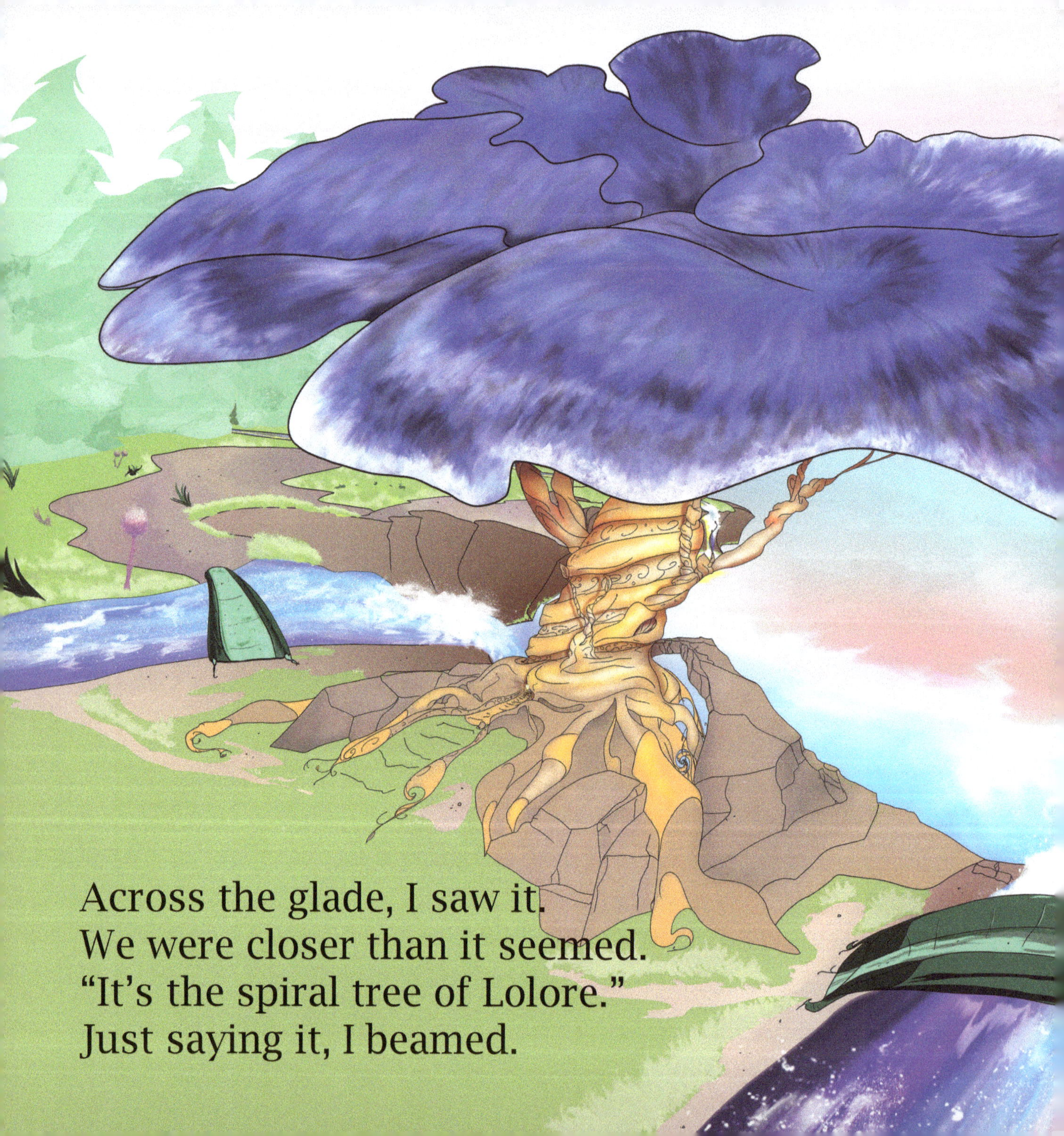

Across the glade, I saw it.
We were closer than it seemed.
"It's the spiral tree of Lolore."
Just saying it, I beamed.

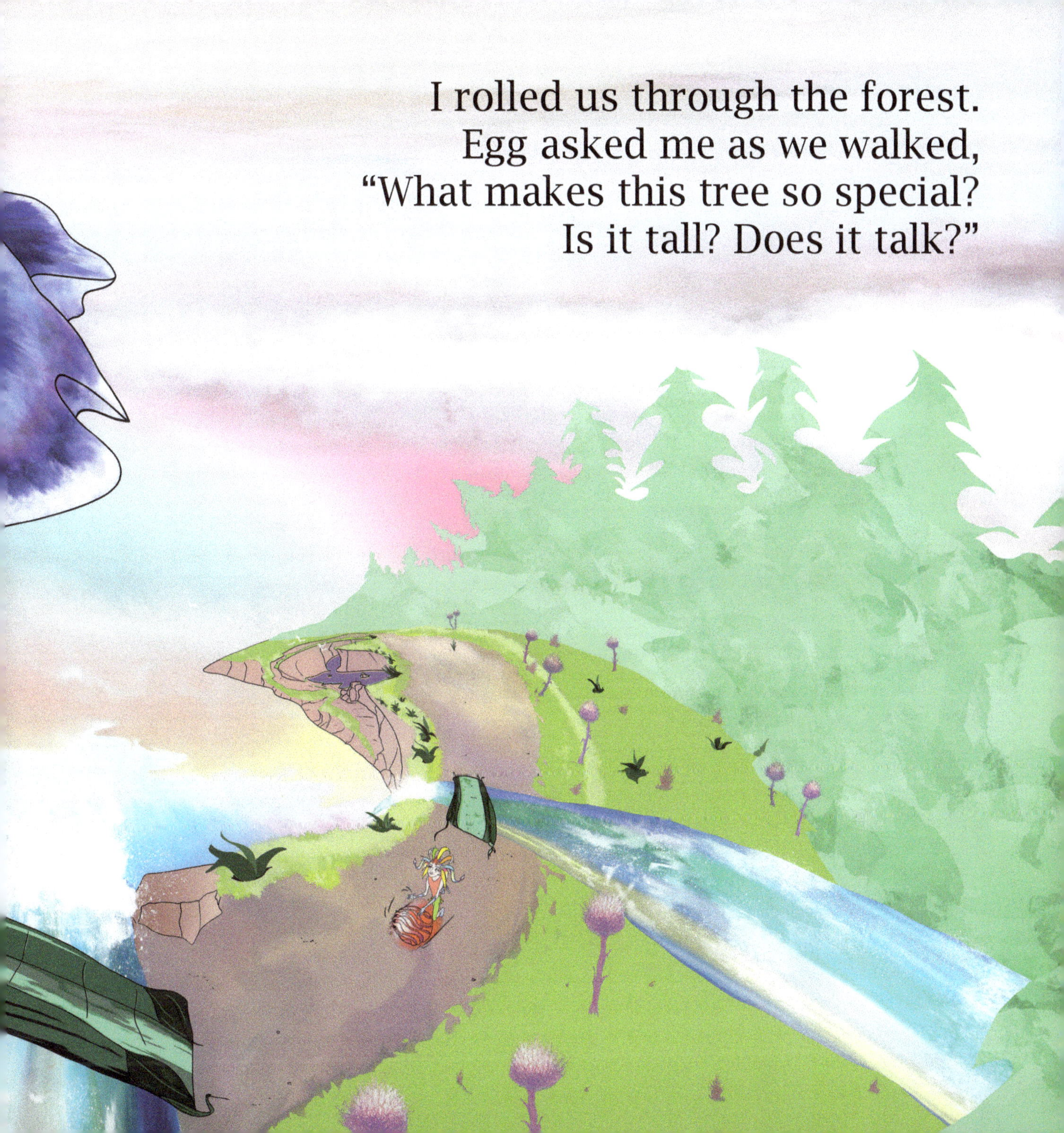

I rolled us through the forest.
Egg asked me as we walked,
"What makes this tree so special?
Is it tall? Does it talk?"

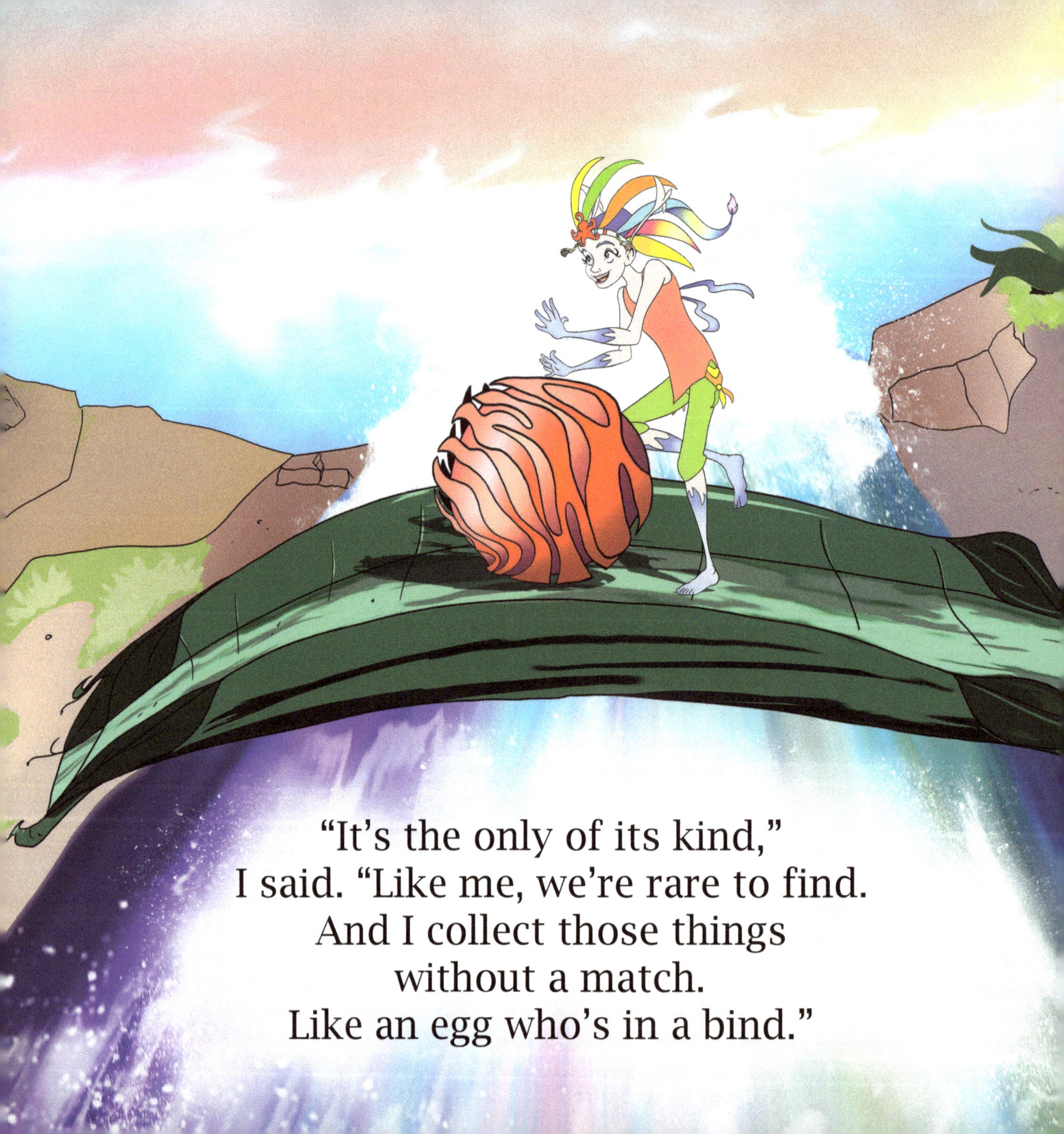

"It's the only of its kind,"
I said. "Like me, we're rare to find.
And I collect those things
without a match.
Like an egg who's in a bind."

Egg laughed, "I like you, Lolly.
I'm glad we met each other."
I smiled and said, "Hey, once you've hatched,
come back and meet my brother."

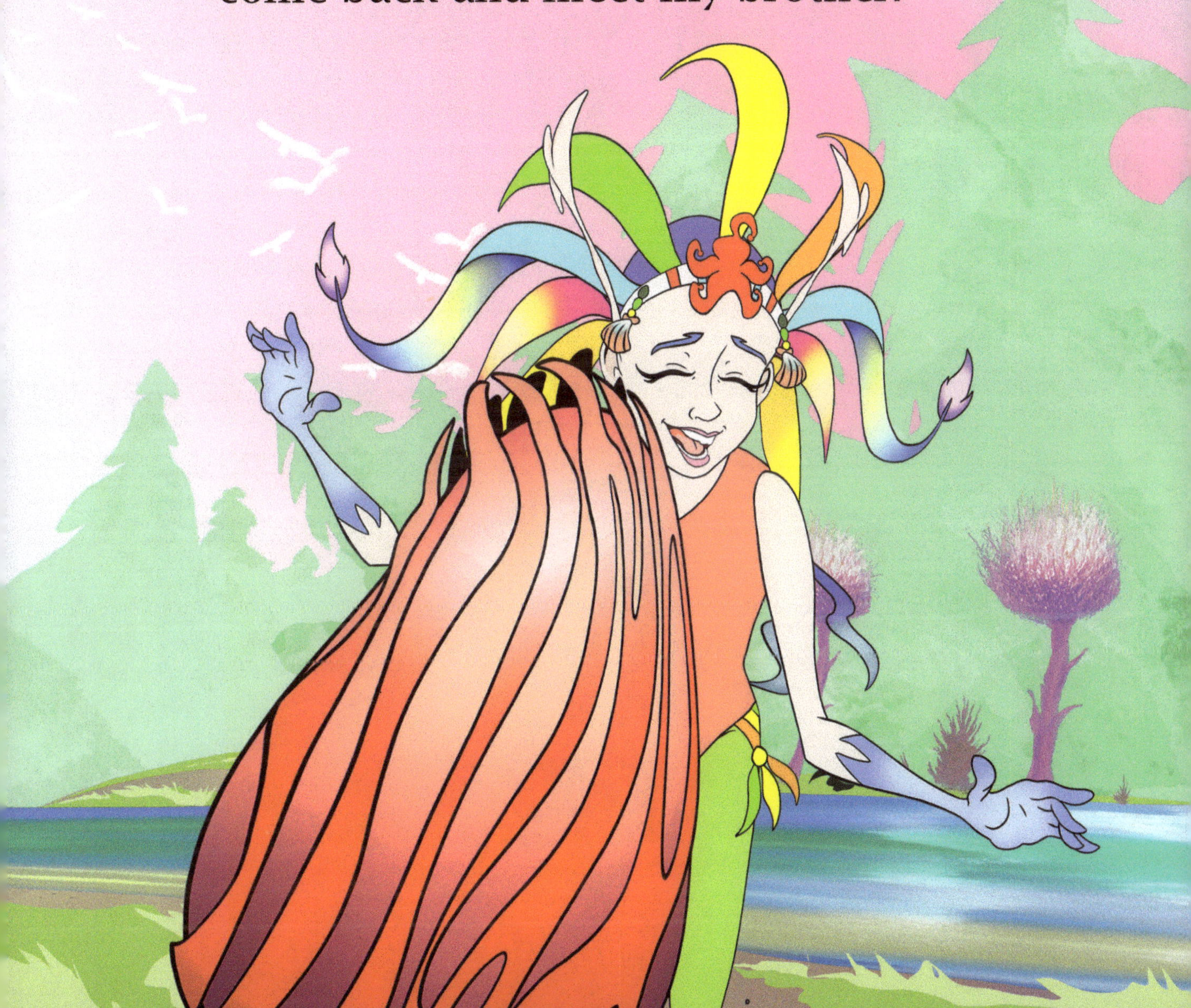

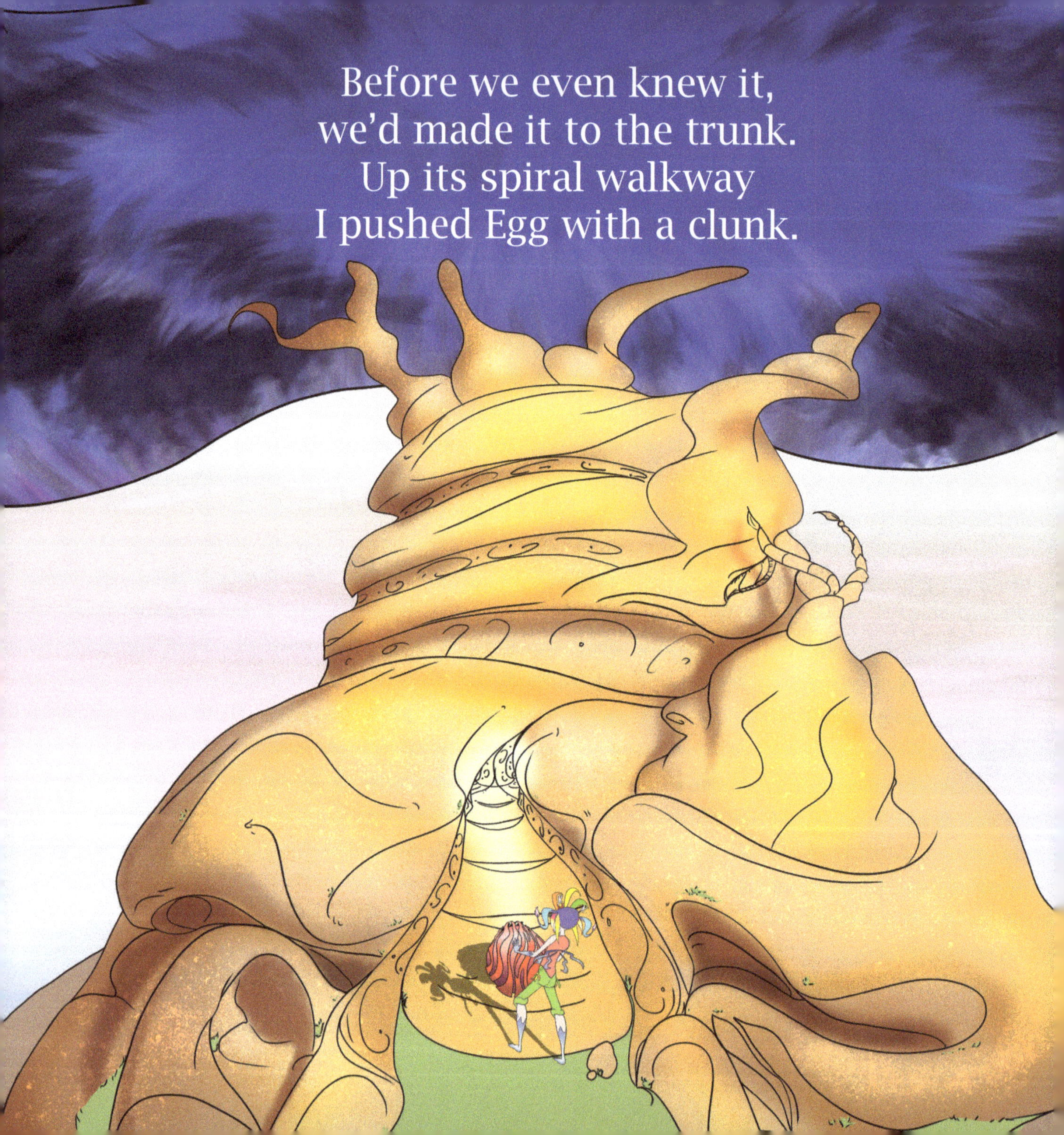

Before we even knew it,
we'd made it to the trunk.
Up its spiral walkway
I pushed Egg with a clunk.

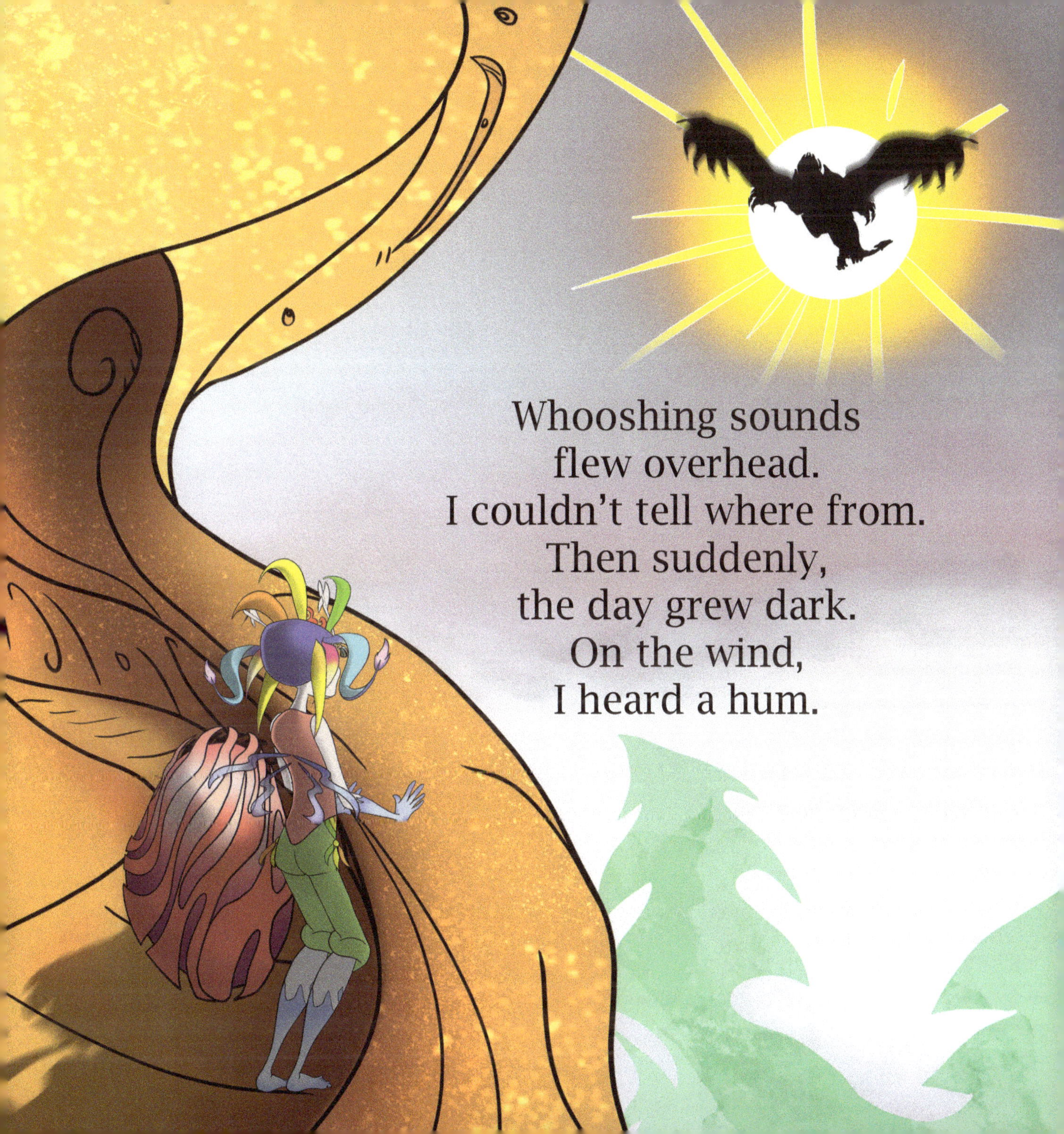
Whooshing sounds
flew overhead.
I couldn't tell where from.
Then suddenly,
the day grew dark.
On the wind,
I heard a hum.

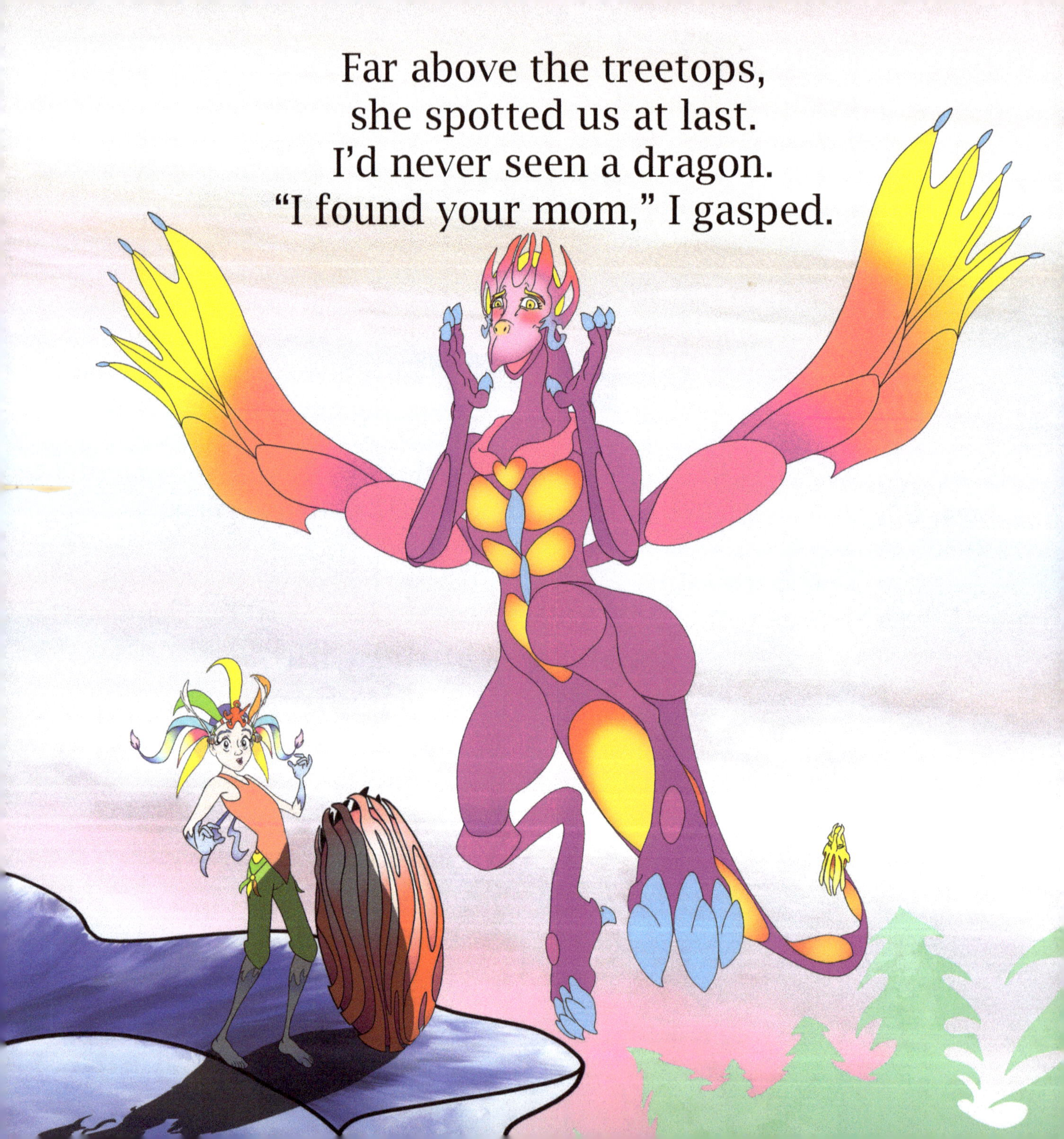

Far above the treetops,
she spotted us at last.
I'd never seen a dragon.
"I found your mom," I gasped.

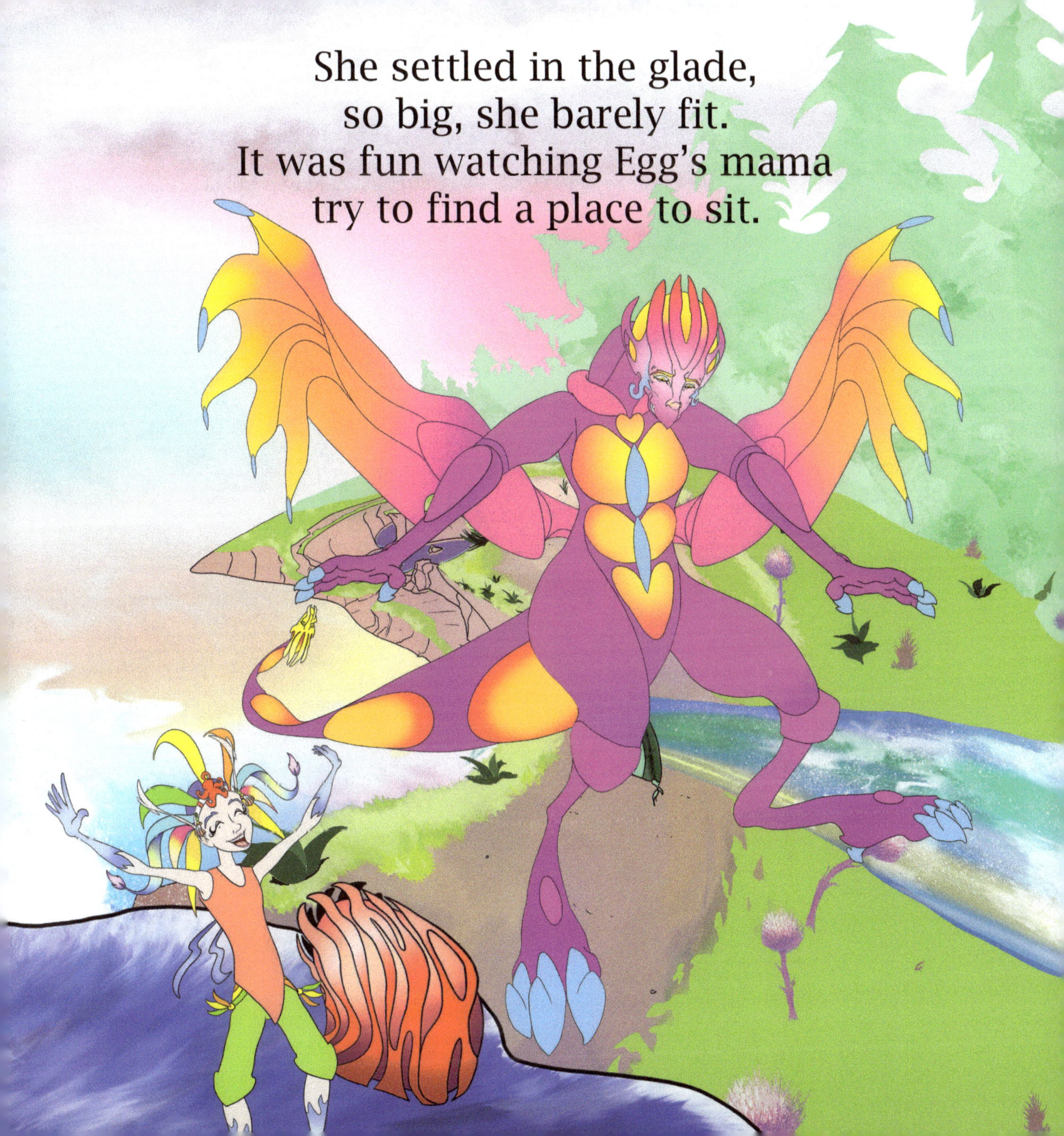

She settled in the glade,
so big, she barely fit.
It was fun watching Egg's mama
try to find a place to sit.

"Oh, thank you, little fairy,
for finding my son, Schnoodle."
The dragon's voice was awfully loud.
It turned my bones to noodle.

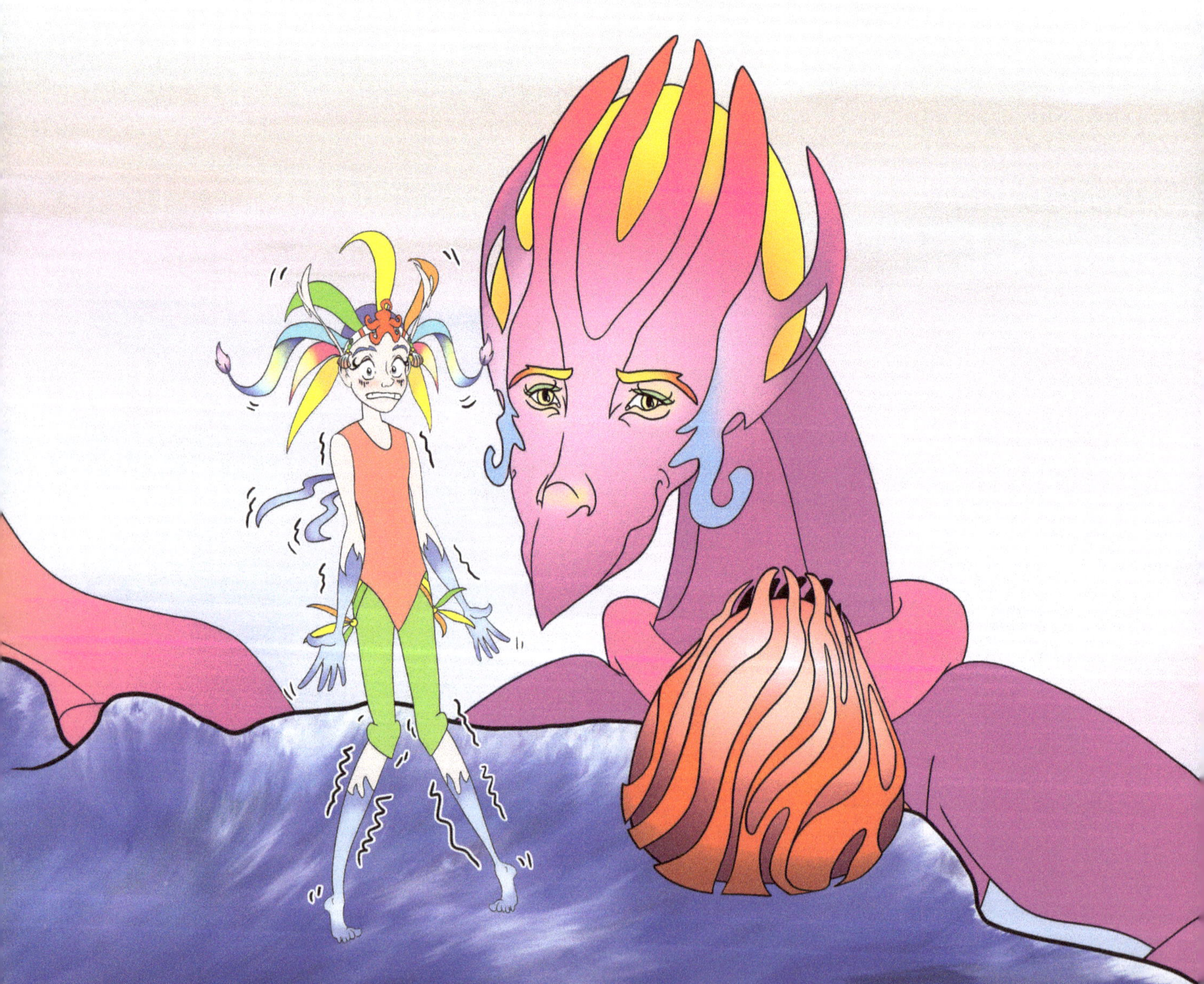

"You're welcome, ma'am," I bowed my head.
"Our afternoon was grand.
I hope that you will bring Egg back
as soon as he can stand."

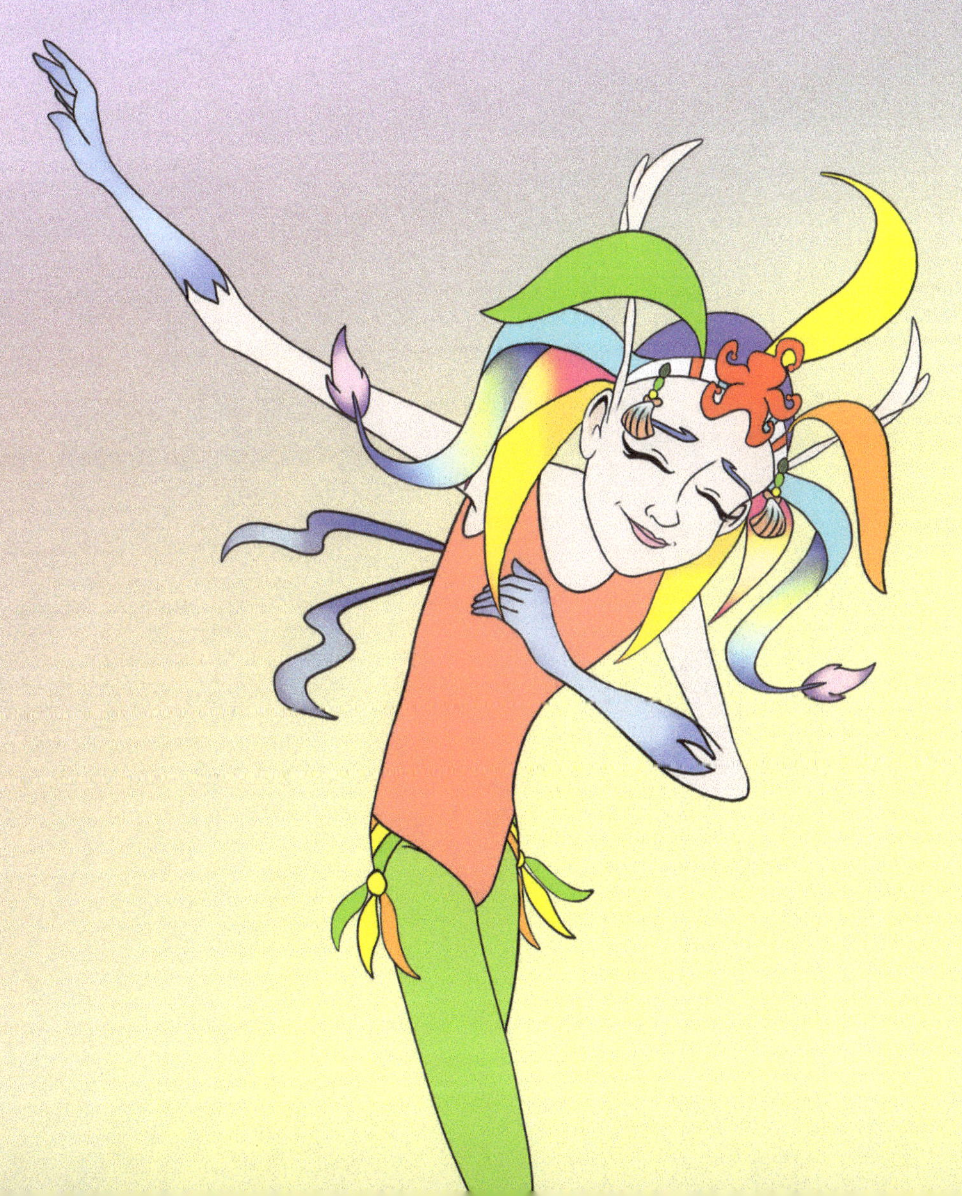

"I will," she said and held Egg tight.
"He was wiggling and fell.
I'm both thankful that you found him,
and for his dragon shell."

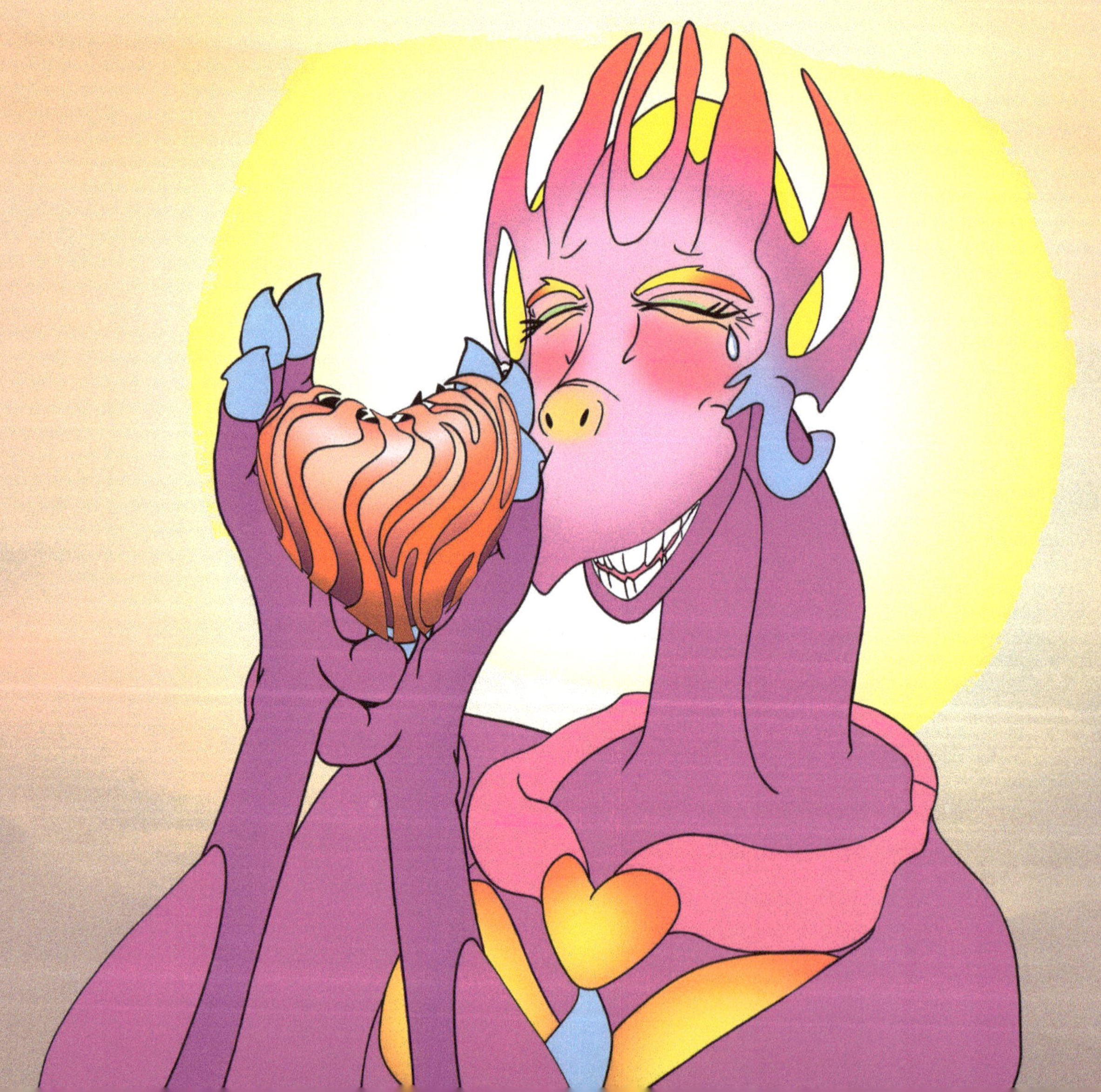

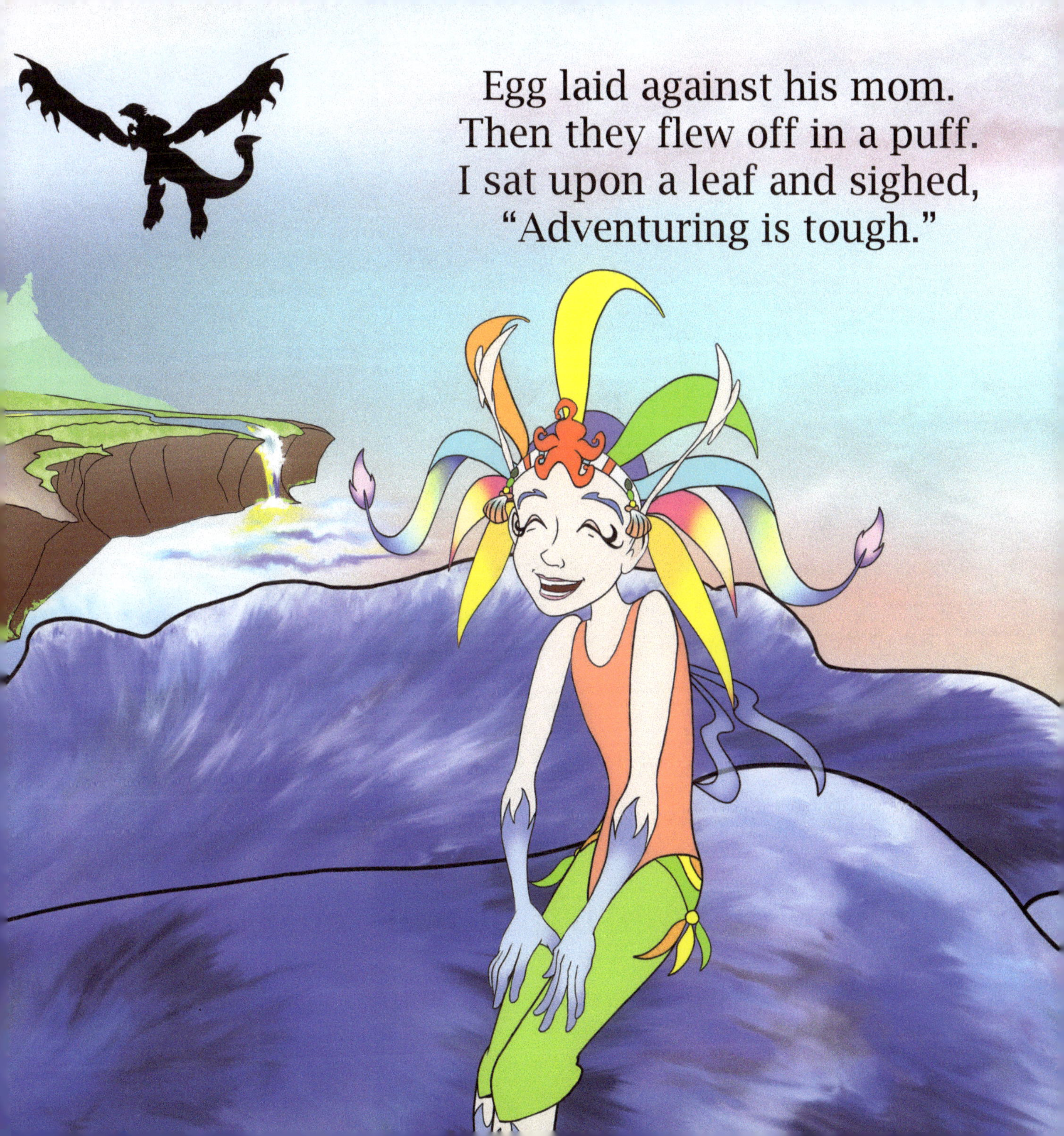

Egg laid against his mom.
Then they flew off in a puff.
I sat upon a leaf and sighed,
"Adventuring is tough."

LOLLYSTOPS

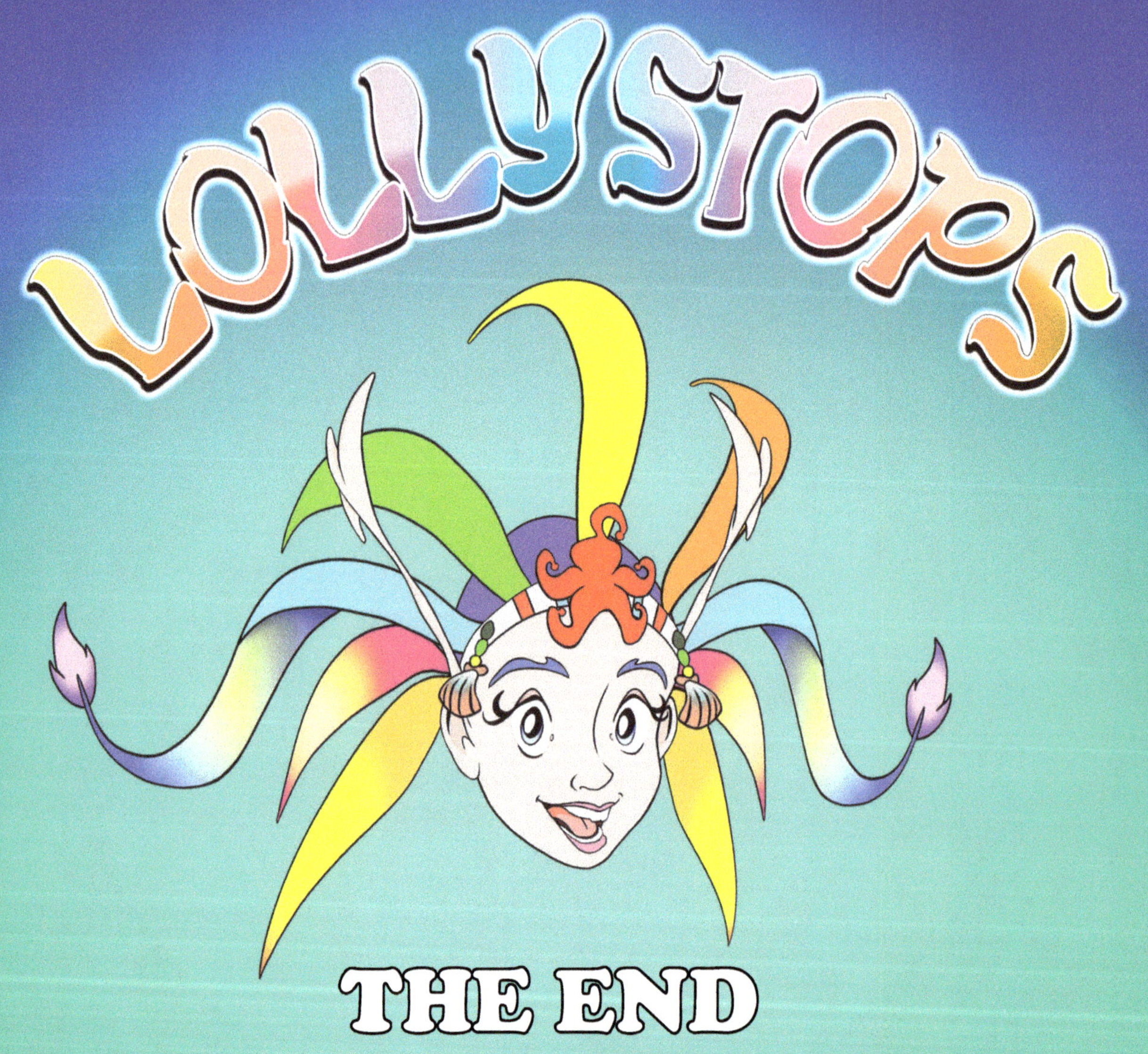

THE END

Thank you for reading my adventure.

And a very special thank you to our LOLLYSTOPS friends
Cindy, Sandy, Valerie, and Liria
for being Lolly's ethereal wings.

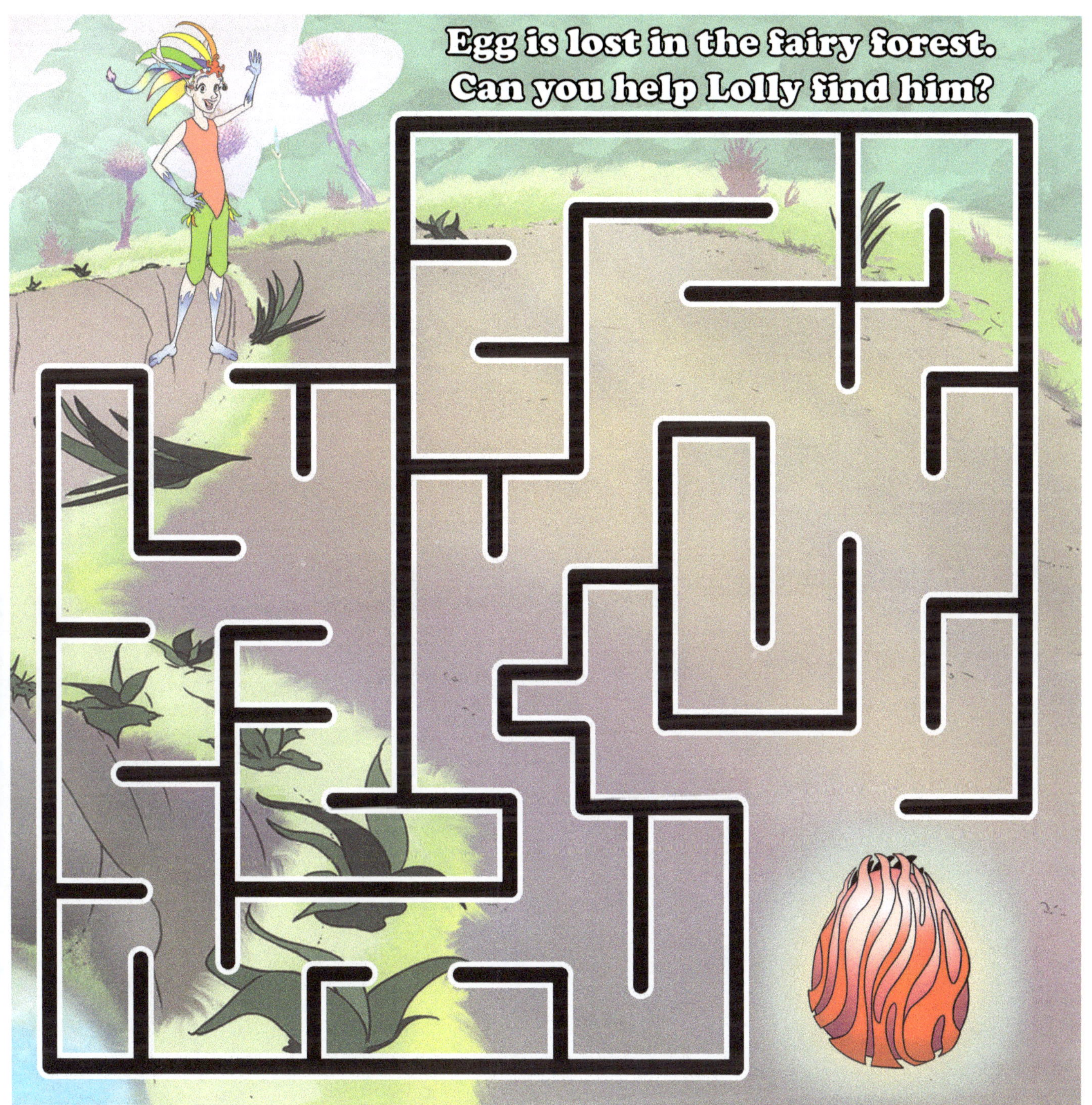

Egg is lost in the fairy forest.
Can you help Lolly find him?
For more fun and adventures visit LOLLYSTOPS.ORG

9 781735 472942